THE
TALENT
SCOUT

ROMAIN GARY

THE TALENT SCOUT

Translated from the French
"Le Mangeur d'Etoiles" by John Markham Beach

HARPER & BROTHERS · PUBLISHERS · NEW YORK

". . . The truth about Faust, my dear sir, is not at all that he had sold his soul to the devil. That is merely a reassuring lie. The truth about good old Faust, and about all of us who are trying so hard, is that there is no devil to buy our soul. . . . All phonies. A lot of con men, impostors, cheap tricksters, fakes. They keep promising, but cannot deliver. No real talent. That's my tragedy as an artist, my kind sir—and it is breaking my little heart."

THE DUMMY OLE JENSEN

THE
TALENT
SCOUT

I

THE FLIGHT had been pleasantly uneventful. Dr. Horwat, who had been looking forward to the trip with some apprehension—it was the first time he had taken a non-American line—was forced to admit that, given a chance, those people were learning fast. He had always been a strong and vocal supporter of American moral and economic aid to underdeveloped countries and, deeply convinced that all God's creatures were potentially equal, he was delighted with the smooth landings, the quality of service and food, and the courtesy of the ship's captain, who addressed the passengers in excellent English to point out the different landmarks and keep them carefully briefed on the progress of the flight.

There had been an unscheduled stop at some airfield in the southern peninsula, where a strange, squat lady with strong Indian features, and dressed in scarlet silks and brocades, boarded the plane. The stewardess explained in a respectful whisper that the lady was General Almayo's mother, who was making her usual yearly flight to the capital to see her son and, as it was generally known that the airline was owned by Señor Almayo, this unexpected interruption of the flight had been accepted by the passengers with good grace.

Dr. Horwat sat next to a young man in an expensive blue silk suit with overpadded shoulders, a brownish face and a childish expression, who spoke very little English. The evangelist tried his Spanish on him. The young man was apparently an artist of some sort, a citizen of Havana, Cuba; he was flying to the capital to take part in some shows there. When Dr. Horwat tried sympathetically to make out in what field of artistic endeavor the young man exercised his talents, his neighbor looked embarrassed, uttered a word in English that sounded, strangely enough, like "superman" and, though this did not enlighten the evangelist much, to avoid a deeper and probably inextricable involvement in language difficulties, he merely nodded in approval and smiled pleasantly, and the young man flashed back at him a remarkable set of gold teeth.

This was the preacher's first visit to the country, and he was coming as official and personal guest of the government. Dr. Horwat, although still in his early thirties, was a very famous man, and quite aware that his reputation as a tireless and inspired crusader against sin and evil in all its forms had been lately quickly expanding far beyond the frontiers of America. He was tall, good-looking and blessed with prematurely graying hair—it helped a great deal to make his youth less noticeable. He could pack the largest auditoriums in the country with thousands of fervent and exalted fans, who listened to his thunderous denunciations of the devil in a state that some of his critics called "mass hysteria" or even "hypnotic trance," and sometimes even went so far as to describe him as a sort of "white Hitler."

He could hold the fervent attention of his audience for hours, and this was not merely a passing spell: long after he had finished, the faithful remained stunned by his thunder, and crowded around him, kneeling and praying and chanting their love of God.

Only a month ago, preaching at the Polo Grounds, he had experienced with profound humility a moment of real triumph: the attendance was larger than that of the

Johanssen-Patterson fight, and the gate receipts were the highest in the Grounds' history. He was in the process of becoming the greatest box office attraction in the country.

Though he considered himself modest, he was not a little proud of this achievement. The fans of God had given him more applause, as he was delivering his inspired vocal blows and punches against the powers of darkness, than to any other fighter in the whole history of the Polo Grounds —and for this he expressed his gratitude in quiet prayers every evening, together with his wife and seven children.

His enemies denounced his theatricality, his flamboyance, and, although they all recognized his talent and what they called his "magnetism," they perfidiously claimed that he was merely a master of histrionics, that he was nothing more than a tremendously gifted performer who could have made a great career for himself on the legitimate stage.

Dr. Horwat was a rather short-tempered, even impatient young man, and sometimes he was not above shrugging his shoulders with an expression of scorn. The fact was that these criticisms hurt him deeply, for he was quite aware himself of a certain theatrical strain in his personality, of his love for large, attentive, eager and admiring audiences. Before opening prayer, as he stood in the pulpit, towering over the crowd, he often experienced an intoxicating feeling of mastery, of power, and he basked in applause, although he always tried to remind himself, as it rose toward him, that it was addressed to God. But whatever technical and perhaps theatrical skill he possessed and employed was dedicated to the greatest cause; it was impossible to lift the spirit of the audience and make a hundred thousand hearts beat in unison without a certain amount of showmanship; and so he did his best. And if he was blessed with that talent that made even the simplest words sound as if they were full of a new, unsuspected meaning; if he could, with one intonation of his voice, make thousands jump to their feet and roar their approval, he never forgot why his talent had been given to him, and he used it to the utmost for the glory of the Giver.

He was now coming to this country for the first time to preach and he knew that it was in dire need of his words and help. The capital had one of the worst reputations for sin in the whole Western Hemisphere; it was a center of wide-scale dope traffic, of prostitution, of gambling, and he even heard that most abominable movies were openly shown in certain theaters.

He was looking forward to his crusade here. He always enjoyed a good fight and he believed in attacking the enemy in his very stronghold. The language would be a difficulty, for it was a Spanish-speaking country, but they must have learned some English at least, catering to the tourist trade. The young evangelist was hopeful that he could overcome this obstacle, and he knew that it was actually the quality of his voice, some strange, compelling power in it, that subjugated his audience and not so much the words themselves.

He had once more chosen as his theme the devil, his true and physical presence in this materialistic world. It had always been one of his most successful themes, one that allowed him to reach the peak of his poetical inspiration, and he believed in it completely. He considered it a great, a tragic mistake, even a crime, of the so-called civilized world to dismiss the devil as a mere symbol—even some misguided churchmen were not above committing this heresy —it was a crude error to consider his existence as a mere superstition transmitted from medieval times, as a mere figure of speech.

Young Dr. Horwat had devoted his considerable energy and a great amount of time to fighting this skeptical attitude. Over the radio, on his weekly television appearances, in hundreds of articles, he had never ceased to thunder home the notion that the devil truly existed, that he was roaming the world, an eternal and villainous prowler, and if it was true that he could take different forms and appear in different disguises, the fact of his presence could not be denied.

The response to this campaign was overwhelming and it sometimes came from unexpected quarters. Contributions for his crusade, financial help to re-establish the devil as the actual living and always present menace to the world, poured in from poor and rich alike, as if the preacher had hit upon some deep fear or craving in their souls; but even Dr. Horwat was amazed when a very large sum of money was presented to him by General Almayo's public relations firm in the United States. He knew that Almayo, or "General" Almayo as his countrymen had automatically begun to call him, although he had never been granted nor had requested the rank of general, was a powerful and even menacing figure. He had even heard him described as a dictator; however, there seemed to be some exaggeration in that.

There were constant attacks against him in the American press, claims that the government and the President of the country were merely puppets in his hands; and, granted these were often inspired by political exiles, the evangelist had nevertheless felt a certain reluctance in accepting the money, and even discreetly consulted the State Department. He was told that to reject the contribution would be interpreted as a deliberate insult, that it would deal a bad blow to American relations with the most powerful figure in the area. And then Dr. Horwat had never considered any man to be beyond redemption, and if this generous gesture meant anything, it was that Almayo had been impressed by his crusade and that the preacher's solemn warnings and appeals beseeching all people to remember that the devil truly existed had touched in this man's heart some responsive chord and some fear of God.

And those who knew the place well had told him that General Almayo had accomplished a lot to modernize the country, that he had built a telephone system which was the best anywhere outside the United States, new roads, schools, a ministry of education, a new university, and had made the place safe for both American investments and for American travelers.

At the airport there were no usual customs and passport formalities and Dr. Horwat found himself conducted respectfully by an airline official to a black Cadillac waiting for him. He observed several travelers who had been granted the same courteous and preferential treatment, and there were other black Cadillacs just like his own waiting for them.

He shared the car with a pleasant, very blond pale-blue-eyed gentleman with a lively and ironic face, who introduced himself as Agge Olsen, a Danish citizen from Copenhagen. Dr. Horwat noticed that he was holding a rather large and peculiarly shaped box on his knees instead of stowing it, for their mutual comfort, in the baggage compartment. And then there was the young Cuban also sharing the car with them; he had modestly settled himself next to the uniformed driver.

The airport was a good hour's drive from the capital, which was surrounded by volcanic peaks and, as the car started, Dr. Horwat experienced a sudden oppressive feeling and a certain difficulty in breathing. They were nine thousand feet above sea level, and he had been warned to avoid physical exertion, but any discomfort he was experiencing was more than compensated for by the almost cataclysmic grandeur of the landscape. The capital was hidden somewhere far away behind a volcano that had destroyed it twice in past centuries and, although it was now extinct, its crenelated, snowcapped peak still showed its white teeth in a threatening and savage willingness, and the seemingly endless plain of black lava rocks, dwarfed shrubs and pyramids of stones extending to the left of the road suggested some incredible ruin of the sky. To the right a forest of cacti twisted its petrified anger up the slopes of mutilated rocks, and Dr. Horwat decided that those dry, sun-drenched wastes must be pullulating with snakes.

"Get me out of here!" a voice suddenly said.

Dr. Horwat started and looked toward his companions with some astonishment; but the Danish gentleman was still smiling and the Cuban boy glanced at them with obvious surprise.

"Get me out of here, I said," the voice repeated, angrily. "I am suffocating."

Then there was a cough, but it did not come from the Dane, nor from the driver, and the Cuban boy was looking almost scared.

"Listen," the voice said. "If you don't give me a breath of fresh air, I'll never speak again, and you'll starve."

"What on earth is this?" Dr. Horwat asked.

The Dane appeared intrigued.

"I wonder," he said.

"You wonder?" the voice shouted, mockingly. "Now, Dr. Horwat—I hope I got your name right, sir—I want you to know that you sit next to a tyrant who has been exploiting me for years, riding my back, so to speak. Slavery I call this, my dear sir—exploitation of a unique talent. There should be a law against this, that's what I say."

The box on the Dane's lap suddenly opened and a dummy emerged from it, sitting up.

A ventriloquist, the evangelist thought, with some irritation.

"Meet my friend Ole Jensen," the Dane said.

"I do hate ventriloquists," the dummy observed. "Pleased to meet you, I am sure."

Dr. Horwat smiled wanly. He disapproved of practical jokes—he didn't have that sort of sense of humor. But he tried to be a good sport about it and even shook hands with the dummy. It stared at him with its glassy eyes and the usual cynical expression ventriloquists always feel compelled, for some reason, to choose for the faces of their dummies.

Mr. Olsen explained that they were booked at the local night club, the El Señor—it was said to be one of the best places of its kind in the world, and it often presented new attractions even before the Paris Lido or Las Vegas. The evangelist had never been to the Paris Lido or to Las Vegas, and he felt quite sure that he would not visit the local night club either, whatever its fame. He politely asked Mr. Olsen about his act and the faraway places he had visited on his travels.

"We have been touring the world for almost a year now, away from home," Mr. Olsen said.

"Yeah," remarked the dummy, "and I've had enough of it. I long to go back to his wife."

The evangelist thought the joke rather off color. The Cuban boy was laughing. He was an artist too, he explained in broken English. Mr. Olsen asked him if he was booked at El Señor, and the boy shook his head.

"No," he said, "no."

"And what sort of act are you performing?" Dr. Horwat asked out of sheer courtesy.

The boy's English seemed to fail him suddenly. He had a certain talent—he was well known back in Cuba—and he was booked to perform here, in the capital. Then he appeared unable to find his words, and looked away.

Dr. Horwat listened absent-mindedly as the ventriloquist talked about his travels, while the dummy stared at the evangelist's face with its cynical and unpleasant grin.

"I take it you are yourself an artist?" he suddenly heard Mr. Olsen ask him. "Wait, don't tell me anything, let me guess. I pride myself on being a physiognomist. I can almost always guess the nature of a performer's act by his appearance. Let me see. . . ."

At first, the evangelist was too shocked to protest and then, as he saw the ventriloquist's eye wander with an appraising expression over his face, he became painfully aware of his long white hair, of his piercing dark eyes, of his commanding and striking features.

"An illusionist," the Dane said at last, "a magician or perhaps a hypnotist. Am I wrong?"

Dr. Horwat swallowed hard and told the man that he was a preacher. The dummy gave a croaking, mocking laugh.

"A physiognomist, indeed!" he exclaimed. "All you are, Agge Olsen, is a bloody fool, and I have always said so."

The Dane apologized profusely. It was just that they were all artists here in this caravan of cars. He gestured back to the Cadillacs following them. They were all booked for the new show at the El Señor—he hoped to be forgiven.

Dr. Horwat was considerably surprised to learn that all of his traveling companions were vaudeville performers and apparently, like himself, General Almayo's house guests. He felt annoyed and bewildered. He wondered if this apparent coincidence had been entirely unintentional, or if there were perhaps some quite insulting irony behind it. He had not expected to be General Almayo's house guest. He thought that he would be staying at one of the American hotels in the capital. But when the airline official had told him that General Almayo expected him to stay at the Residence, he did not know what to say, even though he did not like it. And now it was even more disturbing, and even a little humiliating, for a man of his calling to find himself, along with some circus performers, the house guest of a man whose reputation did leave much to be desired, even though he had been recently and with great publicity proclaimed the benefactor of his country. Yet some good could come out of it and he decided to speak freely to his host about some of the licentious and despicable things that were going on in the capital. And then tomorrow, in the largest public hall of the city—the symphony orchestra hall—he would shoot his bolt of lightning against the evil presence that still disgraced the earth.

II

IN THE FOLLOWING CAR, a tall, good-looking man in his forties, with a short, peaked black beard and a mustache, was speaking with a certain sadness to his companion, a smartly dressed little fellow with dyed hair that carefully left only distinguished touches of gray on the temples, who was listening absent-mindedly.

"I am not seeking this for myself," the tall man was saying. "It is not that I care that much for personal glory. True, like all artists, I am not completely indifferent to posterity, although I have seen enough in my time to realize the vanity of public acclaim and the little consolation there is in the knowledge that one's name will live forever. But I would like to do this for my country, for France. We are no longer, alas, the great power we used to be—and I feel that it is more than ever the duty of every French artist to surpass himself. I know that I have it in me—but somehow, at the last moment, it never comes off. Of course, no one in human history has ever achieved this."

"Some people say that the great Zarzidje, the Georgian, pulled it off during a special performance at St. Petersburg, in 1905, under the eyes of the Russian Tsar," his companion said.

"It is a legend," the first man said emphatically, and his face took on a hurt expression. "No one was ever able to prove it. I don't want you to think that I am chauvinistic— but let me tell you one thing: if ever there is a juggler capable of performing his act with thirteen balls, it will be a Frenchman—simply because I will be that man. No doubt you are aware that I was presented with the Cross of the Legion of Honor two years ago, for outstanding services rendered to the prestige of France abroad, for my personal contribution to the display of our national genius. If only once—only once—no matter where, no matter before what audience—I could better the record of the great Rastelli and juggle with thirteen balls, instead of my usual twelve, I would feel that I had truly accomplished something for my country. But I am not getting any younger, and although I am still at the peak of my powers there are moments—why deny it?—when I begin to doubt—and there is a time limit on all of us."

His companion nervously fingered his bow tie. He was the head of one of the greatest talent agencies in America, and for forty years of his life, before reaching his present eminence, he had been a talent scout, traveling endlessly around the world. There was no circus, no music hall, no night club that could claim a new act that he had not visited in his perpetual search. He had long ago reached the top of his profession and had now other talent scouts working for him, but he was still constantly on the road, like an old hunting dog who could not resist following a trail—and although he was becoming a little skeptical with the passing of years, and liked to pretend that he had seen everything the world had to offer, that everything had been done and could only be repeated, under this disguise of detachment and disillusionment his curiosity and sense of wonder were as keen as ever. He still secretly hoped that some unique and superhuman talent would suddenly manifest itself in a remote corner of the earth. He was always ready, at a moment's notice, to jump into a plane and race around the globe to see with his own eyes if it was true that there was a man in Iran who could turn three somersaults leaping into the air and then turn three more on his way back to earth, or if it was true that a fellow in Hong Kong could stand, his head down, his legs up, supported only by his little finger—not the index, like the Swiss artist Kroll and two or three others who had already accomplished this—but on his little finger, a wholly unprecedented feat, an inspiring and heart-warming achievement and a re-assuring proof that there was truly no end to the wonders which humanity would someday accomplish on this earth—that mankind did not dream in vain.

"Santini, the Sicilian, was pretty good," he said.

The Frenchman—his name was Monsieur Antoine and he came from Marseille—looked hurt.

"You know perfectly well that Santini juggled with only nine balls and that he died broken-hearted because he had never been able to catch the tenth," he said.

His companion nodded.

"Yes," he said. "But you must remember in what position he used to juggle. He stood on one foot on a champagne bottle, with the other leg balanced behind him with three rings in continuous rotation around its calf, with another bottle on his head, and two large rubber balls on top of it, while at the same time juggling with nine balls. I remember it well—although of course there were variations. It was an extraordinary act. It is true that he died broken-hearted, but some people say it was because his wife had left him for a lover."

"In my opinion," the Frenchman said with some irrita-tion, "all this business with bottles, all this deliberate choice of a seemingly impossible position while juggling, was noth-ing but an excuse. It was intended as a smoke screen to hide the fact that Santini had never been able to juggle with more than nine balls. He was clever enough to know his limitations and so he worked out a routine to distract the attention of the audience from it, by standing in what appeared to the public as a most precariously balanced position. I don't want to criticize a distinguished artist and a colleague who is no longer with us, but in my opinion Santini was merely cheating. It is true that I myself perform standing with both my feet on the ground, but then I juggle with twelve balls. Who else can do it? It is a classic act accomplished in the purest style, without any cheap tricks to lure the public's eye away from real difficulty. I am a classicist. I am true to the great French classic tradition of the eighteenth century. Purity of style, that is what matters. It is just that I wish that I could catch that last ball."

"You are already the best as it is," his companion said soothingly. "Right now you are the greatest."

The Frenchman sighed. The words "right now" awoke in him the fear latent in every artist's heart that someone, somewhere, suddenly will appear triumphant on this earth and be the first to accomplish the impossible.

"I think I will have another try tomorrow," the Frenchman said. "But I would hate to succeed when I am alone and then perhaps not be able to do it again when the world is watching. You know how incredulous people are. They never believe you. They always have to see it with their own eyes."

"You'll make it someday," Charlie Kuhn said. "I am sure you have it in you."

Monsieur Antoine stared gloomily at the black lava stones piled up on both sides of the road.

III

CHARLIE KUHN's real name had once been Mejid Kura—he was born on the shores of Syria of a mixed Lebanese and Turkish ancestry—but after his arrival in America as a young and eager immigrant, more than forty years ago, and after his first contact with the world of show business, he had Americanized it to Charlie Kuhn—only to find out one day that the name was not perhaps truly typical of everything American. But then it was too late and he was stuck with it, as he was stuck with many other things: his heart, that had now developed a certain murmur; his loneliness—somehow, in his endless rush from one continent to the other, he had never been able to strike up anything more than a brief passing acquaintance with women, even though he was very generous and always willing to pay. And then there was that old, strange, sometimes almost painful and disturbing hope, or longing, or curiosity—he didn't quite know what it was—that kept him permanently in an uneasy state of suspense and expectation, always on the move, on the track of something that in moments of sleeplessness or despair he was often tempted to acknowledge as a mere dream. In spite of his studied display of skepticism, an attitude traditional in his profession, in spite of all the cheap tricksters, phonies, charlatans he had seen in his day—all those parasites of the deep human craving for the supernatural—he had kept his sense of wonder and his faith intact, and was still looking around him with keen attention, always ready for the impossible to happen. He had discovered some remarkable artists in his lifetime, and he remembered them all, their names, their faces, their acts, their troubles and problems, and he knew exactly all that had happened to them and where he could find them, long after they had passed from the public eye. He had a true respect for talent and although none of the great and famous that he had known had ever fulfilled the strange longing that lived in him, for the best among them were nothing more than freaks or hard workers with a limitless patience, he was grateful to them even for the few seconds of illusion they had to offer. And so he listened to Monsieur Antoine's sad recital of ambition and failure with sympathy; it was a story he had heard a thousand times, the bitter and humble tale of a man's dream of perfection. From time to time he glanced at his watch impatiently. It was a long drive from the airport to the capital: it would take another twenty minutes to Almayo's Residence, and he was in a hurry. He had some important news for his friend and boss —it was Almayo who had given him financial backing, and still owned seventy-five per cent of his talent agency. He looked at the motorcycle escort that preceded the caravan of cars, and suddenly realized that since they had left the airport he had seen hardly any traffic, and yet on his previous visits the road had usually been jammed with cars. The only transport he had noticed this time were lorries of the usual soldiery that one always saw around, in their green uniforms and German helmets: after the First World War, the country's armed forces had been trained by exiled German officers, and through all the political changes and upheavals the uniforms had remained the same and the troops still paraded at goose-step, as in the good old days. There was either a big fiesta or, more likely, a political rally: attendance was always compulsory and it inevitably emptied the countryside, reducing all life to a standstill. He lit a cigarette and listened absent-mindedly to Monsieur Antoine's fervently expressed dream of mastery and of proud accomplishments for the glory of his native land and of all mankind.

IV

IN THE THIRD CADILLAC, Mr. Sheldon, the distinguished
American corporation lawyer, who was handling the legal
side of Almayo's business in the States—a chain of hotels,
some oil wells in Texas, and heavy stock market investments, aside from dozens of other carefully chosen and
always sound interests—was sharing the seat with a young
man of medium size and nondescript appearance, except
for long, carefully groomed dark hair and beautiful hands.
The lawyer knew that he would have very little time for
his business discussions with Almayo, that the man would
refuse to look at papers and dismiss it all with the usual
"Okay, okay, you do what's best," before taking him to the
bar for a few drinks and then to dinner and the usual evening at his night club with some strange girls and in rather
embarrassing company. Mr. Sheldon was still trying in his
mind to reduce everything he had to tell him to a few
simple words, and this was not very easy. When he saw
that he was to share the car with another man, he felt a
little annoyed, for it meant conversation and he wanted to
concentrate on what he was going to say. But he did exchange a few necessary banalities, for courtesy's sake. The
man introduced himself as "Mr. Manulesco," and then
looked at the lawyer as if expecting some sign of recognition or encouragement. Then he added: "Antón Manulesco,
the famous virtuoso."

The lawyer thought it a little peculiar for a distinguished
artist to introduce himself as "famous" but he merely bowed

his head politely. He then inquired if the maestro was giving a concert at the capital's new symphony orchestra hall, perhaps.

Mr. Manulesco looked a little embarrassed and sighed heavily.

No, he was giving his performance at the El Señor night club. The lawyer managed to avoid an excessive display of surprise, but he did raise an eyebrow. He then thought it proper to show some interest and asked what sort of instrument the maestro was playing—but he still wondered secretly how it was that a famous virtuoso was performing in a night club.

"I play the violin," the man said. He had just given concerts in New York and in Las Vegas. He had the greatest act, he confided with a sudden and unexpected burst of pride. Just the greatest. In fact, there had never been anything like it. He had perfected it after many years of hard work, under the guidance of his parents, who were also musicians. He was the only virtuoso in the world today who could play the violin—yes, the most difficult pieces of classical music—while standing on his head.

He looked at the lawyer, obviously waiting for an exclamation of wonder and some mark of respect. Mr. Sheldon, for a few seconds, stared at him fixedly in utter amazement, then swallowed hard and managed at last to utter some words of esteem.

Mr. Manulesco acknowledged them with a brief nod and then went on describing his act in great detail. True, when he performed, his head didn't actually rest on the floor, he had the proper support for it in the form of an inverted cap. There was no one else in the world to duplicate this act, for it was not only a matter of balance: the music was what mattered. Of course, there were always those who claimed that the public merely applauded the acrobatic feat—there are envious people everywhere. But even if the audience didn't realize it entirely, what really reached them and made them jump to their feet and applaud was the quality of his music. He had been a pupil of Enesco and he could stand comparison with the greatest. Unfortunately, the public taste had become perverted and commercialized, and in order to promote oneself and get the proper backing, one had to find something striking and new to command attention—that's why he had perfected his act. But he was only twenty-four and as soon as his reputation could be properly established—and it was now only a matter of one or two years—he would revert to the legitimate and classical style of performance and show them what he could really do. He was already successful enough to have been able to acquire a Stradivarius.

The lawyer had by now forgotten his mental preparations for the business meeting with José Almayo completely, and was absorbed in a rather shocked and even pained contemplation of the virtuoso's face. The idea of a man standing on his head and playing classical music on a Stradivarius to a night club audience somehow depressed and worried him. Indeed, he felt appalled. As the young man went on with his explanations, the lawyer experienced a feeling of intense sympathy and even of pity. Apparently, Mr. Manulesco had been a child prodigy—his parents, professional musicians from Rumania, had taught him the violin at the age of four, and he was touring America and giving concerts at the age of six. He became quite famous between the ages of six and eleven. But then somehow, when he was twelve years old, he seemed to have lost the public's ear. There was absolutely nothing wrong with his playing, he added quickly—it was every bit as good as it had been before. It was just that the public lost interest in him. Or maybe he had been badly managed. In fact, the family soon fell on hard times, financially speaking. It was then that a particularly bright and sympathetic agent gave them the idea—and it turned out to be a very good one. He was still only twelve years old and could still be taught to do almost anything; his father and the agent began to train him and within a matter of months he showed remarkable progress. It took two or three years to perfect the attraction and he was back before the public, playing the violin standing on his head, in music halls, circuses and night clubs. It was, as he said before, only a temporary thing—now that he had the public's ear again, he would soon be performing at Carnegie Hall in New York—it was only a matter of time.

The lawyer wondered if the young Mr. Manulesco truly believed what he was saying. Apparently he did. It was quite obvious, from the expression of his smiling, happy face, that he could already see himself playing his Stradivarius before the cognoscenti of New York—and standing on his feet once more, not on his head. He told the young man that he would certainly make sure to be there and to enjoy the performance.

Naturally, Mr. Manulesco explained, he knew better than to take his priceless instrument with him on this particular tour—he doubted that there would be anyone in the audience able to grasp all the finer subtleties of his art —and, anyway, for this particular night club act, he had had a special violin made for him, a miniature violin. It took great skill to play, for instance, the Enesco Concerto on it and the night club public was always more impressed by technical skill and showmanship than by the music itself. He carried the violin with him right here, in this bag

—he showed an expensive leather bag at his feet—together with his costume. No, he did not perform in traditional tails; he usually wore white stockings, slippers and pantaloons, and a beautifully embroidered vest glittering with green, pink and red sequins.

A musical clown, the lawyer thought, with a sudden sadness.

The driver was watching respectfully in the rear-view mirror the wrinkled face of General Almayo's mother. She was chewing mastala leaves which she carried in an American-made handbag on her knees, obviously a present from her son. She was a Cujon Indian from the hot tropical jungle valleys in the southern peninsula, and she couldn't read or write. The driver, although he was wearing a civilian suit and a plain chauffeur's cap, was a member of the special Security Force and he knew why General Almayo brought his mother once a year to the capital: he had himself photographed with her and it made him popular, not only with the Cujon tribes, but with all simple people everywhere, including in the States. It showed him as a man proud of his humble origins and it was a very democratic thing to do.

"Yes, I suppose you can call me a fighter," Dr. Horwat was saying in answer to a comment from his Danish companion. "A fighter against evil."

"Kayo in the first round," the dummy quipped, staring at him from the ventriloquist's knee. "I could give you a good tip, Agge. I could tell you how to place your bet."

The caravan of cars was now approaching a roadside café —a shabby and dilapidated place under the black mountain slope, with the faded name of an American soft drink still visible on its walls—the only reassuring sight in this wilderness. They had already passed it when the driver brought the Cadillac to a stop so brutally that Dr. Horwat was projected against the forward seat and suddenly there were soldiers on motorcycles and jeeps everywhere, spread in a semicircle across the road and facing them, while an officer climbed down from one of the jeeps with a swaying radio aerial over its windshield and walked toward them. The evangelist noticed with some surprise that all the soldiers were carrying Tommy guns in their hands.

V

THE CAFE was so squalid inside, so downright filthy, that Dr. Horwat was surprised to see a brand-new telephone on the bar. The place was empty, but through a window in the back the evangelist caught sight of two figures, a man and a woman, running away barefooted toward the rocks on the mountain slope; as they ran, stumbling and falling once or twice in their evident panic, the man kept throwing scared glances back toward the café and the soldiery, and then darting forward once more with lightning speed.

This struck Dr. Horwat as very strange, but it was even stranger to have been stopped so abruptly, if not brutally, on the road by armed troops, and almost pushed into this distressing place. The others had crowded around the officer in charge—a short, squat man, with pock-marked cheeks and a brutal, unpleasant expression on his face, but who was polite enough and was trying to appease them. He was merely carrying out his orders, he explained, raising both hands to request silence; he was Captain García of the Security Force, and he hoped that they had had a pleasant journey. He had been told, over his jeep's radio, to interrupt temporarily their drive and await further instructions—but just then, he explained with a shrug of his shoulders, either his radio gave out—they were checking it right now—or, more probably, something went wrong with the transmitter at headquarters. So he had taken the liberty of bringing them here and he asked them to make themselves comfortable while he tried to reach his commanding officer over the telephone. He was very sorry—just a technical hitch—and then he stepped behind the bar and proceeded to pour himself a very large glass of liquor, which he emptied instantly. Then he grabbed the telephone and dialed a number.

"I wonder what it's all about," the evangelist said to a man with a little gray mustache and bow tie, who was leaning next to him against the counter.

"There must be something going on, on the road ahead of us, that we are not supposed to see," Charlie Kuhn guessed. "Perhaps some police action against the students —they're always rather self-conscious and shy about those things. You can't exactly call this a democratic country, you know."

"I am quite aware of that," the evangelist said dryly.

The door to the café had been left open and he saw another Cadillac come to a stop, with two heavily armed motorcyclists on both sides of it.

"Those are special security troops, not ordinary police," Charlie Kuhn said, rather uneasily. "They're under General Almayo's personal and direct command."

A girl stepped out of the car and, after a brief argument with one of the soldiers, walked toward the café. Dr. Horwat knew instantly that this was an American girl. Her face had a familiar and open niceness that brought a pleasant smile to his lips. She was every inch a college girl from back home, and looked as if she had come here straight from the campus. But then he became aware that she was more than a little drunk; she remained a moment standing in the doorway, one hand against the wall, with a defiant expression, and then walked toward a table with greatly exaggerated steadiness and sat down.

She was very pretty, with delicate features and a sweet,

slightly upturned nose, a lovely, full mouth and short, almost boyish brown hair. She took a pair of glasses from her pocket, put them on and looked around, then put them back into her pocket again. She could not be more than twenty-five years old and Dr. Horwat felt that she should not be sitting there alone with such indifference and so obviously drunk.

Captain García appeared to know the girl quite well and, taking a bottle and a glass, he came from behind the counter and put them on the table in front of her, bowing with evident respect and saying something in Spanish. The girl shrugged and then filled the glass to a level which caused Dr. Horwat to raise his eyebrows. She drank half of it and looked at them again. She seemed to notice Charlie Kuhn for the first time and raised her hand in a friendly gesture of recognition.

"Why, hello there," she said. "What are we doing here?"

Charlie Kuhn walked over to her table and spoke to her.

"I wish I knew," Dr. Horwat heard the girl answer. She was talking very loudly. "It seems to be just one of those things. I was staying with some friends in the country and these boys walked straight into the house in their usual gloomy way, and told me to come along. Oh, well, José will soon have it all fixed."

Charlie Kuhn glanced over at Captain García, whom he knew as one of José Almayo's most trusted men. The Captain was now busy with the telephone. The agent left the table and walked back toward Dr. Horwat with the quite evident intention of overhearing the conversation.

"Who is this girl?" the evangelist asked.

Charlie Kuhn glanced toward the table.

"She's General Almayo's . . . fiancée."

The word "fiancée" came out rather unconvincingly, and

Dr. Horwat was aware of it. He felt quite upset.

"Is she . . . American?" he finally asked with a faint hope that he had been wrong after all.

"American," Charlie Kuhn said. He was listening to Captain García's conversation with somebody on the other end of the line.

"Excuse me," the officer was saying. "I don't think I heard it correctly. Can you repeat it, please?" He remained silent for a moment; then his eyes widened and he swallowed hard.

"Shoot them? Did you say shoot them all?"

"My Spanish isn't too good," Dr. Horwat said amiably to Charlie Kuhn. But his companion appeared to have suddenly frozen.

In his effort to avoid all possible misunderstanding, Captain García had raised his voice, and the girl had overheard him. She said, with a trace of boredom: "Oh, God!"

"Did you say to shoot them all?" Captain García repeated once more.

He knew the voice of Colonel Morales perfectly, but he wanted to be absolutely sure.

"Yes, shoot them all."

"But . . . Excuse me, sir, there are some American citizens among them. . . ."

He gave a quick glance at the dark-haired woman who was sitting at a table chewing mastala leaves, with her elegant American handbag on her knees.

"And there's General Almayo's mother, of course," he said, respectfully lowering his voice.

"Wait a moment."

Everybody in the café, even the ventriloquist's dummy, had his eyes glued to Captain García. The lawyer, who spoke Spanish fairly well—some of his best practice was in

Latin America and the Caribbean—was ash-gray. For one brief moment, Charlie Kuhn hoped that this might turn out to be another of José Almayo's practical jokes, but he did not manage to convince himself. He took his handkerchief and wiped the cold sweat from his face.

Dr. Horwat's Spanish suddenly improved considerably, but of course he knew that this was impossible. He could not have heard it right. He had never been very good at foreign languages.

The Captain was speaking again. "Yes, sir."

"General Almayo says you can shoot his mother too."

García took off his cap and put it on the bar. With his free hand, he grabbed the bottle and poured himself a drink, while still talking respectfully.

"I beg your pardon, sir, but for an order of such importance, I would like to hear it from General Almayo himself."

"You just do what you are told. General Almayo is busy with more important matters."

The Captain drew a deep breath. He threw another quick glance at the old woman, grabbed his glass and emptied it.

"More important matters, sir?"

"Yes."

García wiped his mouth and his face with his sleeve. He looked scared.

"If I am to shoot the General's mother, sir, I would like to hear that order from the General himself."

"The General is busy on another line."

Captain García now appeared to be close to tears.

"All right, then," he said. "It's all right about General Almayo's mother, if he's busy on another line. I'll carry out the order. I'll shoot her. It's his own mother after all, so I suppose it's all right. But what about the American citizens?"

"You just put them against the wall and shoot them immediately. You understand, García? Immediately."

"I'll do it, sir, you may be assured," Captain García cried out. "I've never yet refused to carry out an order. It's just that for an order of such a particular and national importance, like shooting American citizens, I would like to hear it from General Almayo himself."

"All right, you fool, the General is now busy on another line. Hold on."

García held on. With the other hand he grabbed the bottle and pressed it against his lips.

"The best goddamn telephone system outside the United States we have here," the girl said, in a loud, drunken voice. "I should know. I was responsible for it. I made them build it, and the roads, and the symphony orchestra hall, and the public library . . . and then . . ." She began to cry. "He's such a bastard, really."

They all stood there in complete silence. Even the ventriloquist's dummy appeared stunned, fixing Captain García on the telephone with his glassy eyes. Then Dr. Horwat began to roar. He raised his voice to such a thunderous pitch that Captain García winced and waved his hand angrily.

"Silence, silence," he said in English. "I can't hear."

Dr. Horwat was truly giving his best. Words like "international law," "human decency," "unheard-of bestiality," "devastating reprisals," "devilish knavery" were simply flowing from his lips. He even made a very rare thing with him —a regrettable pleonasm, speaking of "impudent cheek."

The dummy, firmly held in his arms by Agge Olsen,

turned his head toward his master.

"The man has real talent," he said. Then he looked toward Charlie Kuhn. "You should sign him up, Charlie," he said.

The Captain was still waiting with the receiver pressed against his ear. He was deeply aware of the historical importance of what was going to happen. This would be the first time in history that American citizens were to be shot in the country. Not murdered—that had sometimes happened in the past, when the country was not safe for travelers—but legally shot, on official orders.

He suddenly stiffened to attention.

"Yes, General, sir," he said.

He recognized Almayo's own voice on the other end of the line.

"You hear, García? Shoot them all! Shoot them immediately, you ass! And then report here at once."

"Yes, sir," García said, waiting for the bang at the other end before putting his receiver gently down. Then he looked at them. He was already considerably drunk and what he saw made his eyes almost jump out of their sockets. In front of the little group of cowed and petrified travelers now stood a white, green and pink scintillating ghost in wide pantaloons, with a thickly powdered face under a pointed hat, and holding a miniature fiddle in his hand.

"What's that?" Captain García shouted.

It was only little Mr. Manulesco, the famous virtuoso, trying to save his skin. When he had begun to realize the fate that was awaiting him, his mind, running in circles like a trapped mouse, hit on a strategy. He knew that there was some mistake here, some incredible and fantastic error. Whoever could seriously think of putting a musical clown before a firing squad? Maybe the others were spies, but he himself was only a musical clown, and he was going to prove it to the officer. He was going to convince him.

He had grabbed his bag and tiptoed into a lavatory at the back of the café, and there he had changed hastily into his costume and powdered his scared face. Now, with the miniature fiddle in his hand, he stood before the monster with an imploring smile.

"Look, General," he said, "look at me! I am only a musical clown. I did no harm at all. Why shoot me? Think of your children, General. They would love to see me. I would make your children very happy, General. Do you want me to play a little tune?"

"That's what I call a clever psychological maneuver," the dummy quipped.

Mr. Manulesco had broken the spell. They all began to speak at once.

"We are great artists, internationally known," Monsieur Antoine shouted. "You will never get away with this."

"Get me the American Ambassador on the phone this very instant!" Dr. Horwat roared.

"If you dare, I'll make it my business to see to it that you hang for this," the lawyer shouted, with a certain lack of logic.

"Let me talk to José Almayo," Charlie Kuhn was saying. "I have important news for him—he's waiting for me—it is very important."

The Cuban boy was standing silently in a corner. The American girl left her table and, taking her glass, went over to the Indian woman.

"Do you remember me, Mrs. Almayo?" she asked her in Spanish. "I visited you a few months ago with José. Do you remember me?"

The old woman stared ahead of her, chewing and smiling

happily. She was completely absent, in a state of mastala-induced stupor.

"Oh, dear," the girl said, with a sigh. "It's such a difficult country. But I love it. I love this country. And I've done a lot for it. One day, I'm going to have a street named after me, or perhaps even a monument, just like Evita Perón. I just love this country and its people. But they are such bastards, really."

Captain García raised both his hands in a commanding gesture. After all these years of routine police work, as one of General Almayo's most trusted officers, he still could not resist a certain feeling of importance when he was about to command a firing squad. It was not that he enjoyed killing people, but there was a silent moment before he gave the final command when he felt suddenly immensely wealthy. It was as if he were inheriting the earth. The sun, the land, the trees, the volcanoes, everything was becoming his. His father and his grandfather were bandits and they killed people to take whatever they happened to have in their pockets. But he was taking more—he was taking the whole world—and when he barked his final command, life always hit him like a strong drink.

He observed them for one more brief moment with solemn eyes.

"You are all going to be shot now," he announced.

"But why? Why?" the evangelist roared. The girl touched his arm reassuringly.

"You must understand that this country is very different from ours," she said, "and we have not yet succeeded in educating them."

Captain García walked from behind the counter and bowed slightly.

"The American citizens first," he said, in a gallant if

somewhat drunken tribute to the good-neighbor inter-American relations.

As none of them moved, the guards began to push them with their rifle butts toward the back door. Agge Olsen held his dummy firmly in his arms.

"Stage call," the dummy quipped. "This is a capital moment, so let's do our best. I knew you were going to get it, one day, Agge. I hate ventriloquists, anyway."

Monsieur Antoine offered some resistance but soon found himself outside in the sun-drenched back yard.

"All right, you swine," he shouted. "I'm going to show you how a true artist dies. Come on, gentlemen, let's sing our swan song. Let's put on our last show. No damned police state is going to silence the true artist."

The Cuban boy was crying. Dr. Horwat, though lost in a thick haze, felt it his duty to console him; then it occurred to him that he knew nothing about this child and he felt compelled to show some interest in him. He patted him on the shoulder amicably.

"Who is this poor boy?" he asked Charlie Kuhn, as they were being lined up against the café wall.

Charlie Kuhn was now far beyond trying to spare anybody's feelings.

"He's the latest Cuban superman."

This struck the evangelist as odd.

"He can perform sexual intercourse an incredible number of times, almost without interruption," Charlie Kuhn said, in a thick, desperate voice. "These freaks are very popular on the blue circuit."

Dr. Horwat was so horrified that he turned his eyes away quickly from the Cuban monster and stared at the firing squad almost with relief. Whatever mistakes he had committed in his life, he now knew he had been right about one thing—the devil truly existed, and it was his hand that was pushing them now against the wall—even if it appeared only to be Captain García's hand.

He felt punch-drunk, that was what it was, punch-drunk. His enemy had pinned him against the ropes and was pounding him with all his might, with everything he had. He saw Captain García pull out his gun and the soldiers grab their rifles, and he tried to say something soothing to the American girl, who was standing next to him, but he heard her say: "I only wish I had done more for this country. I don't mind dying, really, but it's such a negative thing to do. Oh, God, I have been such a failure."

"Look at the truly great artist, you swine!" Dr. Horwat heard Monsieur Antoine shout. He fastened his glazed, indignant eyes on the tall Frenchman standing there with his back against the wall in his shirt sleeves, juggling in a state of noble patriotic frenzy. He saw the Indian woman smiling happily, still chewing her mastala leaves: she was either in a drugged trance, or perhaps imagining that this was some sort of official ceremony of welcome. He saw Mr. Sheldon, the lawyer, in a superb gesture of defiance, swallowing a tranquilizer pill, and this, considering the few seconds they had left to live, struck Dr. Horwat as such a noble, optimistic and wholly American thing to do that the young evangelist raised his head proudly and steadied himself, and felt almost calm, as if the tranquilizer had already acted upon him too, by some miracle of mercy. His eyes wandered to Mr. Manulesco, in his scintillating buffoon's dress, playing on his minuscule violin something that sounded like an aggressively Jewish tune. He heard Captain García shout a command. He met the dummy's attentive eye and heard his mocking voice say: "Kayo in the first round, preacher. I told you so."

He made a frantic effort to wake up and remember the faces of his children, to raise his thoughts to God, but his eyes were still going from the crazy Frenchman, who was juggling, to the musical clown with his face thick with white flour, playing defiantly and almost gaily his Jewish tune, and he heard the ventriloquist's dummy quip once more: "What's death, after all? Nothing but a lack of talent!"

And then the monstrous thought occurred to him that the only artist among them who was not performing his act was the Cuban superman, and that this should be his last thought on earth filled him with such horror that, crestfallen, he turned his eyes toward the firing squad with the awful feeling that he deserved everything that was coming to him.

VI

"JUST FOR LUCK," said José Almayo. He was sitting behind his huge desk under a portrait of the Liberator, his tie and shirt undone, smoking a cigar and playing with his pet monkey, the only living creature that dared to treat him disrespectfully. He loved monkeys. Most people found that they had something human about them, but he thought that there was more to them than that.

At the other end of the room—a hundred and twenty square feet of marble—birds were chattering and fluttering in a spacious cage that reached to the ceiling. Along the walls, on their perches, the macaws and parrots uttered from time to time their piercing shrieks.

The desk was twenty feet long and had seven telephones on it, from one end to the other. Almayo kept them there mostly to impress the American visitors, but this time he wished he had more lines established to his Residence. There were also five open bottles of liquor, two of them empty: Almayo could drink more without getting anywhere than anyone Radetzky had ever known—and he had seen an awful lot of bars in his life.

"Listen," Radetzky said. "You can have your own mother shot for luck, and that won't shake anyone in this damn country. But you just can't shoot American citizens, even to please the devil. That would mean the end."

Almayo frowned. Where he was born and raised, it was bad luck to use the word "devil" like that. It was considered disrespectful and dangerous to pronounce his name. He was always referred to by the Indians, even in the Cujon dialect, as "El Señor." The tradition probably dated back to the days of the Spanish conquest, when the name was carried by those whom the Indians feared and respected most, and who had the power of life and death over them.

"I don't believe you are drunk," Radetzky said angrily, "but I do know that you are crazy. You are cutting your own throat."

The monkey jumped suddenly from Almayo's shoulder onto the Baron's knees. The Baron sat very stiffly, waiting for evolution to catch up with him. Considering, however, the present prehistorical state of the human race, he thought it highly unlikely that this would ever actually happen, and therefore all he could do was to display a completely stoical impassivity and scorn and indifference toward whatever befell him, toward all those disgusting and totally subhuman adventures into which circumstances forced him. He tickled the monkey's ear almost affectionately.

It has been widely held since the days of Darwin that humanity descends from the apes, but considering certain aspects of contemporary history and society, taking into account Einstein, Freud, the hydrogen bomb, José Almayo, dictatorships, gas chambers and mass executions, this seemed to the Baron a preposterous claim, a mere slur on the apes and another false hope fed to humanity. He scratched the monkey's ear and the monkey kissed him on the nose.

Díaz, in an obvious state of terror and nervous exhaustion, his lips twitching, was talking on one of the telephones, and probably not listening at all in his panic, while Colonel Morales, the second-in-command of the Security Force—

the most reliable troops at Almayo's disposal—was putting call after call through to the presidential palace and to the chief of staff.

Radetzky sat in a deep chair to the right of the desk, staring at José Almayo. In spite of the heavy drinking and desperate tension of the last few hours, José's features were still amazingly young and fresh and, in their own way, innocent: there was some indestructible naïveté in him, a total lack of skepticism. In his shirt sleeves and braces, the tie and collar undone, the pistol dangling loosely in its holster, chewing a cigar, he didn't look much different, at first glance, from any other big hoodlums Radetzky had known. But then one became aware how deeply this tall, massive and always strangely immobile and silent figure belonged to the land of black lava rocks, of poverty and superstition, of dead volcanoes and stone gods smashed by the Spanish priests but whose mutilated faces the peasants still kept turned reverently up, away from the earth, toward the sky. Some long-lost drop of Conquistador blood added a touch of sharpness to the strong Indian features. The eyes were gray-green, watchful, and there was not a trace of cynicism or even of irony in their fixed stare, only a keen, attentive seriousness: the oldest dream that had ever lived in a human soul was in him.

Otto Radetzky had been the man's inseparable companion for almost eighteen months, and there was very little he did not know about him. In fact, he knew so much that he was ready to leave him—but, now, it looked as if it were too late.

Things had begun to happen only a few days ago—not dangerously at first, for Almayo always kept a firm grip on the Army and the police. There had been a young officers' revolt in the north and their men seemed to follow them, although this was not yet quite certain. It was a ridiculous attempt—they were barely a thousand strong—and that very morning Almayo attended a government meeting at the presidential palace, where the chief of staff showed him exactly the position of the rebels and of the loyal forces on the map and gave him his word that the little isolated garrison up there in the north would be surrounded and destroyed within forty-eight hours. It was essential to have the matter settled quickly, before news of the absurd attempt could reach the American press, and so a severe censorship was clamped down on press agencies and all foreign correspondents were closely watched.

Almayo drove back to his Residence completely reassured. That night at dinner, he was entertaining some of his business associates from the States and he had arranged for a private performance of the new show opening the next day at the El Señor. He looked forward to the evening with pleasant expectation.

They were back barely a half-hour when shooting started in the streets and the telephone began to panic. The police had revolted, and the chief of police had been burned alive. The Special Security Force was attacking police headquarters and was meeting with violent resistance. Worst of all, the regiments garrisoned in the capital were fighting with each other; the armored regiment had come out for the northern rebellion, while the infantry troops were remaining loyal.

But what amazed and disconcerted Almayo was not the Army revolt—there were plenty of young colonels who were hungry, ambitious and tired of waiting. What truly surprised him were the little people: peasants from the markets, workers, shopkeepers—those who had absolutely nothing to gain in all this. They had turned against him, almost without weapons—he had always taken good care of that—carrying clubs and stones and machetes, and some were even fighting with their bare hands. They were now trying to reach the Residence—thousands and thousands of them, marching with their arms linked, singing and shouting, and although there was very little they could do, the Security Force had to be used against them, leaving the rebellious police and the tank regiment opposed only by the infantry and the Air Force.

The Residence was built on a mountainside high above the city and the windows of the air-conditioned room were closed, but even so he could hear above the rattle of machine guns a wild roar that mounted and receded like some angry sea: the people's voice. It was obvious that he had been treating them too gently, but it was not true that he had underestimated them. It was just that he had always thought himself popular.

Now he listened to the roar with satisfaction: it was bad luck to be loved.

"You just leave it to me, Otto," he said.

"I can't see that the shooting of American citizens can possibly help you out of this mess," Radetzky said.

"Okay, okay," Almayo said, gesturing with his hands as if to appease a child. "So it's not going to help me immediately and personally. But it's going to ruin the boys who are trying to get me. Because let's understand it clearly. It's not me who is having some innocent Americans executed. It is the rebellious Army and the populace and the new government. They got hold of some American friends of José Almayo and they shot them on the spot. See?"

Radetzky gaped. He had long been used to the incredibly tortuous ways of this fabulous, primitive and cunning mind, but this was the best insight he had ever had into its almost mythical strangeness.

"They will deny it," he said, "and it will be easy for them to prove that you have done it."

Almayo shook his head. "It is not going to be easy for them to prove to a nice civilized country like the United States of America that I have ordered my own mother and my own sweetheart shot. People don't go around shooting their mothers—not even in politics."

Radetzky sat there silently, staring at him, trying to look his part: one of Hitler's most trusted paratroop commanders, a reckless adventurer, the dictator's personal military adviser and good drinking friend.

"And then what?" he forced himself finally to ask.

"And then," Almayo said solemnly, "the Americans will land the Marines and they will send their airplanes with bombs and they will just teach these young dogs a lesson—and I'll be back. Okay?"

"I don't know that it's going to work out that way," Radetzky said, "but where will you be waiting in the meantime?"

"The southern peninsula," Almayo said. "Three thousand men there and General Ramón. He's with me. You heard him just now. You talked to him. He's loyal. He has nothing to gain with the others: he is already rich."

"How on earth will you get there?" Radetzky asked.

"The Air Force is still okay," Almayo said. "I'll get there all right. But I am having those Americans shot, just to be sure that I come back with American help."

The monkey had jumped to Radetzky's knees and was asking for attention. The macaws uttered another piercing shriek. The only way in which he could still hope to avoid that incredible folly, Radetzky thought, was to gain time.

"Now, listen to me for once, José," Radetzky said. "Things aren't as bad as that yet. Wait till you see the way the fight is going in the city. It's crazy to have those Americans shot now. You may still win."

"Sure, I am going to win," Almayo said. "I am going to win ab-so-lute-ly. And then I am going to have those dogs tried for mass murder of American citizens, so that everybody knows what dogs they are. They are going to confess everything—you can be sure of that."

Radetzky was speechless.

"I still think it's . . . premature," he said. "At least, don't do it now. Wait. You can have them executed later."

Almayo looked almost pained.

"You heard me give the order, no? You know what happens when I give an order."

"You can call them back and cancel it," Radetzky said.

"Now, that's not the way I feel about myself," Almayo said solemnly. "It's not the way my people feel about José Almayo. I gave the order. They're nice and dead now. And you can't do this kind of thing to American citizens—as those who are responsible will soon find out. So you just take it easy, and have another drink, okay?"

The monkey chattered, and Otto Radetzky felt its little hands searching for fleas in his hair.

VII

TWO MONTHS EARLIER Radetzky had been walking through the gardens of the San Miguel Monastery, on the western outskirts of the capital, where the thick fragrance of roses was so strong that it struck him as if it were something solid. There were pink, yellow and red bushes of them along the wall and white flowers grew through the cracked marble on the ground around the cacti and the *agave* trees. He had requested an interview with the Father Superior and the interview had been immediately granted. They obviously knew who he was—or thought so, anyway. It all had started with a casual remark Almayo had made during one of their drinking bouts. Radetzky had had too much to drink and perhaps he had been asking too many questions. José Almayo had leaned heavily across the table. "If you really want to know how I got this way—what made me big—you go and ask Father Sebastián, at the San Miguel Monastery. Maybe he can tell you. Maybe he can't."

He had been waiting in the patio for quite a while now, stopping sometimes between the arches to look toward the plain, where cypresses stood like some petrified sentries of Heaven. The Indians called them the fingers of God, though it was highly unlikely that God would point a finger at Himself. He had come there in search of some new shred of evidence, to gain perhaps some new insight into the mind and soul of a fabulous man. He had always been fascinated by violence—perhaps secretly attracted by it. Crime had always appeared to him as man's terroristic effort to master and possess life; it was not against the laws of society that the great criminals rebelled, but against a far more powerful and more efficiently enforced law. It took some idealism to attempt it. Otto Radetzky had lived close to some of the greatest adventurers of his time, and he had always been amused by their deep belief in power. He considered himself a cynic. He often angered them by his famous saying: "All you can do is to raise a nice family." He did have a pessimistic streak in his nature. Nothing upset a desperado more than to hear him murmur over a drink: "Now, my friend, in the end, all you can do here below is to raise a good, clean family, with nice, sweet little kids. That's as far as it goes." They were always shocked and dismayed. He undermined their world, their faith, their secret longing. "You believe in nothing," one of them told him—the most famous arms smuggler in the Caribbean, who was now operating in Algeria.

There was a sound of footsteps and the Father Superior walked toward him—a German or a Dutchman, Radetzky decided, glancing at him, as he was led through the long corridors, with bad oil portraits of saints rotting on the walls in the open air, and then taken to his office—an enormous white room with nothing but a large crucifix on the central wall, which underlined the bareness of the place. Perhaps because of the sound of a slowly dripping fountain coming through the window, the peace was much more that of a Moslem mosque than that of Christ.

The Father Superior was seated now behind his desk. He had a yellowish face, blue eyes and a small, reddish Rembrandt-like beard. The marks of age were there in the thousands of wrinkles.

Yes, he said rather guardedly, he had known the General Almayo some twenty years ago, when the latter was a boy in his early teens. He was a Cujon Indian from the tropical valleys—a very proud people, and one of the most ancient of the land. They had had an elaborate civilization there once—if a pagan cult based on human sacrifices could be called civilization—anyway, archaeologists were quite dazed by the profusion of gods they were still digging out almost every year. An old village priest, Father Chrisostomo, had taught him to read and write and then recommended him to the Dominican Order: the boy had a quick mind, he was eager to learn, and it was thought that he could perhaps one day make a good subject for priesthood. The Order paid for his trip to the capital and took care of him there. But it soon became apparent that the young Cujon was very difficult. He seemed to believe in God deeply and yet, for some reason, he would become offended and almost incensed when a teacher reminded him that God was our Master, that all men were His children. He even had wild, vicious fights with other pupils whenever they dared to mention the very simple truth that the good Lord was watching everything that was happening here below: he seemed to take this innocent statement of fact as a sort of slur on our Maker. His teachers admonished him severely, but to no avail. The boy was not to be convinced. He was very stubborn, he had quite obviously made up his mind about many things, and he would stand there in front of the Father Superior, whenever the latter reprimanded him, and stare—just stare—it was never easy to make a Cujon talk. Only once did he consent to explain himself.

"God is good," he told the Dominican. "The world is bad. The government, the politicians, the soldiers, the rich, those who own the earth—God has nothing to do with them. He is only in Heaven."

It must be remembered, of course, that the lot of the

Indians down there in the valleys had always been very hard and no government had ever done much to improve it. But they had learned resignation and accepted their fate. The boy, however, was quite exceptionally bitter. His teachers did what they could for him—they kept trying. Unfortunately, he had soon fallen into some rather undesirable company. . . . The Dominican's voice became a little uneasy, and Radetzky carefully repressed a smile at the Father Superior's evident and sudden prudence. Anyway, José soon dropped out of sight. Apparently, he had become interested in bullfighting and was going from ring to ring, trying to master the art. He had found a protector of sorts—a very wealthy man, who had given him the best trainers—it seemed, however, that he had no talent for the ring and that his perseverance led him nowhere. Father Sebastián kept hearing about him from time to time. He was making new friends—third-rate bullfighters, cheap ring owners, unsuccessful managers—the usual pathetic trash that surrounds a man's dream. Once or twice, the boy had come to see him, and he had tried to warn him— but he was very young, ambitious, and he was also good-looking, which didn't help or perhaps helped certain things too well. . . . Once more the Dominican glanced at his visitor with some embarrassment. This, of course, was long ago, he added rather self-consciously, obviously remembering that he was talking to the dictator's best friend, and it only goes to show that a man can overcome all sorts of difficulties and dangers and reach an important position— that is, if any position in this world can be considered important.

Father Sebastián saw the boy only once more and he remembered the meeting well, for it had been very strange. It was carnival time, and for weeks the capital had been full of laughter; there were bullfights, dancing and firecrackers everywhere. He had left the chapel and was sitting in the empty classroom going over some exercise books. The door opened and a young Indian walked into the room. He was immaculately dressed in white and his shoulders and hair were covered with confetti. But his face was grim. He stood a moment silently in the door, watching his former teacher, then walked toward him.

"Well, José, what a nice surprise," Father Sebastián said.

The young man kept staring at him without uttering a word. It was obvious that he had been drinking. There was something hostile, even menacing, in his attitude, in the tense, animal immobility of his body; he reminded Father Sebastián of one of those figures of stone which still threw their pagan shadows over this supposedly Christian land and over the minds of its people.

"They laughed at me," the boy said. "They threw dirt at me. They laughed me out of the ring."

"Well, any *torero* meets with those things, I understand," Father Sebastián said kindly. "Isn't that part of the profession?"

"Yes, but I've never met with anything else," the boy said. "Never. And yet . . ." He looked at the Dominican almost threateningly. "I prayed so much," he said.

If there was one thing on which Father Sebastián prided himself, it was the strong check he had always exercised over his Dutch temper. But his voice did rise a little and, as usual when he felt irritated, his Dutch accent was heard clearly over the Spanish one.

"A prayer is not a bargain," he said sharply. "It doesn't buy you anything."

Then he softened a little. "Perhaps you were not meant to be a bullfighter," he said. "There are other ways to live."

The boy remained thoughtful for a moment, then shook his head.

"You don't understand. You are not an Indian, so you don't know how it is. If you are born an Indian, you have got to fight. You have to be a bullfighter or a prize fighter, or a great bandit. Otherwise, you go nowhere. They don't give you a chance. Everything is closed, you can't get through. They keep it all for themselves. They have it all fixed. But if you have the talent, even though you are only a Cujon, they'll let you through. They don't mind, because you're only one in ten millions. You can get to the top, have all the good things. Their women, they'll love you, and you can live like a king. But you have got to have the talent. Otherwise, you just rot, there is no way. I have the talent all right. I can feel it in me. When I stand up there, my feet firmly in the sand, with the muleta . . . That's my place. I feel I am a man. I am no longer a worm in the mud. I feel I am alive."

His voice trembled and he clenched his fists.

"But then it doesn't come off. Something happens and it doesn't come off. Everything fails again and there are jeers and hostile cries. Yet I never run away. The bull either throws me or I try again. But in the end the bull always throws me. I have been gored so many times."

Father Sebastián was looking at him over his glasses. He was deeply shocked and sad.

"Have you seen me fight, Father? I have courage."

"I am afraid I am not an *aficionado*," the Dominican said gruffly.

"I will be a great *torero*," José Almayo said defiantly, looking at the priest. "I will have the talent. I don't mind what it costs me. I will make good. I know the price. I will pay it. That is why I came to see you. I wanted to warn you."

Father Sebastián didn't quite understand him, and he just said: "I seem to have been a bad teacher."

The boy smiled; the lips curled suddenly and there was a trace of superiority in the flash of white teeth, and the face took on a slightly patronizing expression.

"Oh, you have been a very good teacher. But you don't know much. You are a good man and so you can't make it out. The world is a bad place, and if you want what it has to offer, you have got to be bad—truly bad—worse than the others, or else the others will beat you to it. The world doesn't belong to God at all. You have to ask someone else for talent." Then he walked away.

Father Sebastián remembered how he sat there for a long while, staring over his glasses, his pen in his hand, at the door that had closed behind José Almayo. The street was still full of noise and among all the screams and shouting and laughing and music and firecrackers, the serpentine hissing of paper rockets sounded like some cynical persiflage. He had suddenly felt an apprehension that perhaps he had not lived up to his task—that he had failed to understand, to help. But the boy had been attending class for barely a year, and there were so many other boys to help, to guide. In later years, when events had so completely confirmed his . . . foreboding, he often wondered why it was that he hadn't fully sensed the despair and the wish to be helped that had brought the young man to him that night. He blamed himself, but he also knew the reason was simple enough and very humble: there had been too much noise in the street and the pagan sounds of the fiesta had irri- tated him and had made him cross. No, he had never seen

José Almayo again, he said, rising from his desk. But, of course, he had heard a lot about his former pupil.

Radetzky was holding the monkey in his hands firmly, to keep it from new mischief, and the creature was complaining loudly, its black little face wrinkled in anger, showing its teeth, and trying to tear at his hair.

"I still think you should try to cancel the order," he said.

"Nothing to worry about. It will work out fine."

"Listen, José," said Radetzky. "No man alive has yet managed to step out of his skin into something better."

"I don't get it, my friend. I am only a Cujon. We are simple people, remember. Just peasants. I'll be okay. Ab-so-lute-ly. Have a drink."

VIII

THE EVANGELIST realized that he was still alive and though he found himself looking into the guns' muzzles, there appeared to be some unexpected hitch in their execution. He glanced toward Captain García and saw him in excited conversation with a soldier who was pointing toward the road. He had come running from behind the house a few seconds before, but Dr. Horwat had mentally taken leave of this earth and he hardly could be expected to notice those who were still treading on it. Captain García shouted a command and the soldiers lowered their weapons. Then the officer made an apologetic gesture toward the prisoners.

"Un momentico," he said politely, as if he wished to reassure them that this was only a momentary interruption and that their execution would be carried out in just a few minutes. Then he disappeared quickly behind the café with the soldier who had come to fetch him.

Monsieur Antoine was still juggling. He was so completely absorbed in his performance and so intoxicated with the evidence of his great artistic skill that he seemed to have risen victoriously above their mortal peril—that is, to have forgotten it—the humble purpose, the merciful delusion of all art. The dummy sat still on Agge Olsen's arm.

"Never a dull moment," he said.

Mr. Manulesco was still playing his violin. A triumphant smile had now broken through the thick smear of white over his face: there was obviously no doubt in his mind that this miraculous postponement of their execution was en-

tirely due to his artistic genius and to the spell of his music.
The Cuban monster, although Dr. Horwat carefully avoided
his eyes, smiled pathetically at him. The only thought that
occurred to the lawyer, Mr. Sheldon, in his state of almost
complete mental emptiness, was that with a little luck the
tranquilizer would now have time to act. The old woman
was still chewing happily. She reminded Dr. Horwat of
the katcina pagan dolls of the Arizona Indians—he had
always thought that those dolls had something evil about
them. Charlie Kuhn was wiping his face with a handkerchief. He now felt fairly sure that they were saved, perhaps
permanently; although what he meant by the word "permanently," with that murmur in his heart and humanity's
general lack of talent as far as immortality was concerned,
he didn't quite know himself. But he had an unfailing
dramatic sense and all his old showman's instinct was tell-
ing him that this time the performers would not fall broken
to the ground.

"Golly, I really thought that this was it," the American
girl said. "I usually don't give in to this sort of negative
thinking, but José is so unpredictable. He is a very confused
boy."

They saw Captain García come running toward them,
shouting something, pushing his gun back into his holster
as he ran, and they heard the screech of tires over the stones
as the Cadillacs and the jeeps shot out from behind the café
and came to a sudden stop in front of them in a cloud of
dust and flying stones. Captain García barked some orders
and the soldiers began to herd them together, pushing them
brutally into the cars. Dr. Horwat was now so adjusted to
the circumstances that he didn't even protest when he felt
a rifle butt against his ribs. He found himself trapped in

the back of a car between the Cuban monster and the American girl; staring into the sarcastic and, it seemed to him, gleeful face of the ventriloquist's dummy, whose master had seated himself next to the driver; he saw Captain García emerge from the door of the café, embracing a load of bottles that would have taxed the capacity and strength of any normal human arms; he saw him run toward the jeep with the floating aerial, hand the bottles to his subordinates, jump in beside the driver, and then the jeeps, the motor-cycles and the four Cadillacs started at breakneck speed over the stony ground without any discernible path, away from the road and toward the mountains. After some fifteen minutes of a crazy, bouncing ride, during which the evange-list found himself several times thrown against that awful Cuban creature, who helpfully supported him in his arms, and against this unfortunate American girl, who was having hiccups and then suddenly went to sleep with her head on his lap, they reached some sort of dirt road, which, by comparison, appeared as smooth as Heaven, and the evan-gelist, leaning back and closing his eyes, let his mind slip into a state of exhausted, stunned blankness.

In the front jeep, driving ahead of them, Captain García, although still very drunk, was trying once more to go over the incredible news and to bring some sort of order to his thoughts. When his sergeant had told him that he had managed to establish radio contact with headquarters, only to learn that the rebellion had broken out, with the Security Force in serious difficulty, and that the Army had revolted and was on the point of gaining control of the capital, he hadn't been particularly surprised, not because he had in any way anticipated this, but simply because he knew that an Army rebellion had always been part of the national heritage and political pattern of his country since the days of the Liberator. He had always been prepared to be tortured and executed himself one day, and as he had had a good life he was not particularly afraid of dying. But he hated uncertainty. He had always been a subordinate, merely carrying out orders, and now, for the first time in his life, he was faced with a situation where he had to show initiative and to act independently. He did not believe that General Almayo's regime was finished, even though the message from headquarters was frankly pessimistic. He just couldn't see a man like José Almayo caught with his pants down. And yet anything could happen, for even the best men sometimes go down under the stupid hand of fate. And the first thing his instinct for self-preservation told him was that it would be pure folly to shoot American citizens while the issue of the fight still hung in balance. If José Almayo won the day, he could then execute the Americans with a clear conscience, and no one would ever know that he had temporarily disobeyed his orders and delayed the execution. And if the Army rebellion succeeded, the best, perhaps the only, chance for him to save his skin would be to hold the Americans as hostages in some hidden spot in the Sierra and then bargain their lives in exchange for a safe conduct for himself. Captain García had several generations of mountain bandits behind him, and this was not very different from what they did when they wanted ransom, and so, true to the family tradition, he had grabbed his prisoners and was now driving as fast as he could toward a secluded place where, as legend had it, his grandfather used to hide with his band of good men. He knew that he could not expect to pass undetected for more than a few days, but even then, if the rebels won, he would still be able to negotiate a safe conduct under the threat of executing the prisoners and thus causing the new government a dangerous difficulty with the great American democracy. He now felt extremely proud of himself, of the quickness of his mind and his resourcefulness, and as the jeep drove along the path, he reached back for a bottle and soon began to hum the latest American tune.

It was now almost an hour since they had left the road. The girl had sobered up, and Dr. Horwat introduced himself. He was not at all surprised that she should have known his name, but she did make some strange remarks that rather disturbed him.

"Oh, yes, I hear about you often, Dr. Horwat," she told him. "José admires you very much. He has even instructed his public relations firm in the States to send him translations of your articles and speeches. He likes what you say about the devil."

"He certainly doesn't seem to have benefited much from my teachings," Dr. Horwat said grimly. "This horrible dictator, judging from our present experience, appears to be himself as close to the devil as anyone I've ever known."

"You can't really call José a dictator," the girl said reproachfully. "It's just a different country and they have a different political tradition, that's all. And he has done a lot of good, believe me."

"I doubt it very much," the evangelist said.

"It's only that he's a little superstitious," the girl said with a sigh. "And, of course, people like you, Dr. Horwat, if you'll excuse my saying so, encourage him a great deal."

The evangelist gave her a crushing look. "I don't quite follow you, I'm afraid."

"Oh, I can make it quite clear for you, Dr. Horwat," the girl told him, firmly meeting his eyes. "For centuries—since the Conquistadors' days—the Indians were taught by illiterate Spanish priests that everything they liked to do was evil. For instance, they had great sexual freedom, you know. But it was impressed on them that sex was evil. And to rebel against their masters was evil too. In fact, only resignation was good—submission—silent acceptance of their fate—that was very good. Everything the Indians wanted—to fornicate, to work less or not at all, to kill their masters and to take the land away from them—all this was very bad: the devil was lurking behind it. Some of them learned their lesson well and began to believe in the devil quite seriously. They are superstitious, primitive people—no one has ever tried to change that. Even José is not an educated man—although he has a brilliant mind, really—very logical. Too logical, in fact. So when you, not an ignorant village priest, but a respected and acclaimed public figure, from a great, civilized, powerful country, when even you assure him that the devil truly exists and still rules the world only too often, he feels reassured and grateful—and so, you see, you do encourage him in his superstitious bad ways."

"My dear girl, I do nothing of the sort," the evangelist exclaimed indignantly. "This is sheer blasphemy."

"Well, Dr. Horwat," the girl said with a trace of irony, "I just wanted you to know."

"You seem to have quite a lot of sympathy for this criminal," the evangelist remarked dryly.

"Sure I do," the girl said quietly. "I've been his mistress for three years now."

Dr. Horwat decided that he would rather let this point pass without any moralizing.

"That didn't seem to prevent him from ordering you to be shot," he said.

The girl smiled triumphantly.

"He's often tried to get rid of me," she said, "but he can't. He can't because he loves me. He hates to admit it, but he does. And you see, he has canceled the order."

"That remains to be seen," the young evangelist said gloomily. "We can still be shot at the next turn of the road. But why should a man kill a woman he loves?"

There was again a trace of irony in the girl's smile. She was quite an intelligent and obviously educated girl, Dr. Horwat decided. It made matters even worse. For the first time he examined her face more closely. It was a lively, even a witty face—yet in spite of her youth there were already unmistakable marks of dissipation.

"Why? You should be the last man to ask such a question, Dr. Horwat. He thinks it's bad luck for him to be loved, or to love. I don't want to hurt your feelings, but people like you made him believe in the powers of darkness, in their great strength, and it just so happens that everything José wants is exactly what, in your own words, the evil genius is said to be able to offer. Power, great wealth and endless satisfaction—vice, if you prefer."

"This is known as heresy," the evangelist said.

"Yes, of course. People used to be burned at the stake for this sort of thing, tortured by the Inquisition. I've been through college in Iowa, I have some information on all this. I have done my best to cure him of his . . . obscurantism."

Dr. Horwat winced. She seemed to have aimed this at him.

"I haven't succeeded very well, as you can see. Except perhaps in destroying myself."

Dr. Horwat's wings opened instantly.

"My dear child, at your age . . ."

"And so," the girl went on without listening, "even though he loves me, he is scared of his feelings for me. He thinks it is a terrible weakness. And he loathes even more the idea of my love for him. Just in case I'll put in a good word for him with Heaven and prevent his success—or his damnation, as you would call it, I suppose."

It was certainly the most monstrous thing Dr. Horwat had heard in his life. Heresy—it could only have been bred in a Roman Catholic mind. It just went to show how far back the Roman Catholic Church still reached into the dark age. He had always been opposed to a Catholic being elected President of the United States, and now he knew how right he was.

"I wish I could speak to this unfortunate young man," he said. "Perhaps I could still save his misguided soul."

She watched sadly the naked, barren landscape of the Sierra across the precipice.

"He has other plans for his soul, I'm afraid."

The night was falling fast. The Cuban monster was snoring.

"Who is he?" she asked.

"I don't know," the evangelist said quickly.

She glanced once more through the window.

"José could have been such a great man," she said. "He truly has it in him. A sort of irresistible, compelling power . . . a magnetism. The crowds always fall under his spell."

The evangelist cleared his throat and stared at his hands.

"I know him so well," the girl said. "I could tell you everything about him."

Dr. Horwat felt that he didn't quite care to know or to listen. But she began to speak, and as the caravan plunged deeper and deeper into the shadows, the evangelist did listen—he could do this, at least, for her—and sometimes it was the only way one could help a human being.

IX

THE COLONEL commanding the Air Force was calling every half-hour, pledging his complete loyalty, but at the same time informing José that he kept an aircraft ready, if he wished—temporarily, of course—to leave the country. José Almayo gave him the order to bomb the rebels: the Army headquarters, the tanks and the people in the streets. Then he called him back on the line, and told him to also bomb the public library, the new university, and the symphony orchestra hall. The Colonel ventured a question; it didn't seem to him that those last targets made much sense.

"The students are barricaded there," Almayo told him, and slammed the receiver down. It wasn't true, but he had his reasons.

The shooting seemed to have toned down and the telephone was operating smoothly and under full government control. He dispatched Colonel Morales downtown with orders to report back to him on the progress of the fighting in the streets, and then took a bottle from his desk and went back to his private apartment.

He found the Indian girl squatting naked on a mat, combing her hair, exactly as he had left her. He always kept two or three of them in his palace, and this one was the best; the others had no spark, no devilry in them. He told her to put some clothes on; he was always disappointed by nakedness and always liked to reach for everything that was out of sight.

Afterward, he lay on his back waiting for his strength

to return. He was no longer thinking about rebellion. He knew he was going to win. He was thinking only about his night club, the one thing he truly cared about. He had owned the place for more than ten years now, and because of his position he had someone else to run it for him, but he was still the boss. He had always booked only the best acts there, the greatest talent the world had to offer, and he remembered them all.

There had been a Dutchman who could be pierced through the stomach with a sword and walk away alive and unharmed. It was a miraculous, hair-raising act, and no doctor, no scientist had ever been able to explain how it was done. It was truly as if the man had some supernatural power, as if it had been granted to him. But the Dutchman had died since, in Las Vegas, when something did go wrong with his act.

There had been the mass hypnotist, Kruger, who could handle hundreds of people at once and make them see and describe historical events centuries old. But there was nothing supernatural there, no magic, and Almayo had known for many years now that there was a scientific explanation for hypnotism. And so he kept the world's best agencies busy, and their talent scouts were constantly seeking new acts for him. He had seen them all. He had seen the greatest dancers, jugglers, trapeze artists, illusionists, and a famous drummer from Haiti, Petit Louis, who could work an audience into a trance and create a feeling of unbearable suspense, as if something were going to happen at last. Almayo had often sat alone through the wee hours of the morning, listening to him, drinking heavily—and waiting.

The Haitian was tireless—possessed by a force that gave his arm the secret of perpetual motion. He would crouch on the marble floor beside his drum, his torso naked and covered with sweat, staring at Almayo with a smile that cut through his face like a twisted white crack. He seemed to know what it was all about, what was eating him, and tried to help. His hands, almost invisible in their speed, beat the drum in endless combinations of sounds and rhythms that never seemed to repeat themselves—a summons, a command, an invocation, almost an order for someone to appear, for something to happen—and Almayo sat there with a dead cigar in his mouth, the beating of his heart answering the beating of the drum, longing—and waiting.

But nothing ever happened. No one ever came, no one ever answered the summons. The Haitian was only the best drummer in the world, and that was all.

José was beginning to be disillusioned by artists. There was no one behind them: they were on their own. They knew how to cheat, how to give themselves briefly an air of mastery, but the real power was elsewhere; they had no access to it. They did not have it in them to pay the price. He himself had paid it many times over. He had become a famous villain; his ruthlessness, his dedication to evil were recognized even by his bitterest enemies; his reputation had grown far beyond the frontiers of his country; shocking accounts of his deeds were appearing almost daily in the Latin American press and could not possibly have escaped the attention of anyone interested in true earthly merit. Since the day when the young Indian boy had first taken a hard look at his native land, seen the poverty and hopelessness in which his people were deliberately kept, the corruption, the injustice around him, with the power secure in the hands of the army and of the police—since he had first come to the conclusion that the world was a wicked place and identified its master, he had always done his worst to prove himself worthy. And yet something had gone wrong, and it seemed now that all his efforts had been ignored. Perhaps he had not been bad enough, after all.

He got up and went to the window again, to watch for the planes. He stared at the new, tall buildings in the heart of the capital, the skyscraper of the University towering above them all. The American bitch, he thought suddenly. It had all been her work. She had probably undone everything he had accomplished, all the proofs he had given of his willingness. He sat on the bed, smoking a cigar, remembering broodingly how he had tried to bring the name of a poor Cujon youth to the attention of those who, as the Spanish priests had so often assured him, were constantly prospecting the world, always on the lookout for fresh talent, for a new and promising soul.

He could see the fat man's face and he could hear him say: "Better luck next time, boy."

He touched José's cheek. It was a soft and yet heavy hand, like a fat iguana, and José knew it well and hated it.

He was still wearing his suit of lights, and the fat man had paid for it, as he had paid for many other things. José no longer believed in the fat man: he no longer trusted him. True, there was something evil about him, about his hands and his exigencies, but José knew now that he was not important enough, not big enough, that he probably did not even have the right connections.

He had promised him a lot, but it hadn't worked out. The arena was empty, but José still could hear the jeering shouts of the crowd, the laughter and the insults, the mocking voices. He still saw their faces, thousands of them. They were still there. He knew that it would take him days, and perhaps weeks, before he could find silence again; the mocking, grimacing faces would follow him for days, and at night there would be no stars in the sky, only sneering faces looking down on him. The fat man had been lying to him. It was not enough to be willing to sell one's body and soul; the difficulty was in getting paid.

He looked at the fat man for the last time. Everything was there: the yellowish, heavy eyes over the dark pouches, the corrupt mouth, both soft and cruel, the podgy reptilian hands with ruby and diamond rings. One truly expected to see behind his back, as Father Chrisostomo used to say, back in the village, "an abyss of darkness and fire, full of twisting bodies and reptiles."

And so he had trusted him. But in spite of his promising looks, the man was obviously a cheat, an impostor, and at best he had only helped him to make a step in the right direction. Now he had to go much further than that.

"I won't be seeing you again," he told him.

The fat man took the cigar out of his mouth. His chin began to tremble. He pressed his hand against his heart and there were suddenly tears in his eyes.

"I'll do everything I can to help you," he said. "Everything. I'll hire the best teachers to train you. I'll buy you the best bulls. We'll go to my ranch and for the next season you will be ready. And I'll buy you a new car."

"I won't be seeing you again," José said. "You are a cheat, a liar. You can't do anything for me. You are not big enough. You are just a fraud."

The fat man was crying. "We'll go to Mexico," he said. "They will train you there. You will be great—the greatest. Don't leave me, José. What will become of you?"

"I'm going back to my village tonight," José said.

"What will you do there?" the fat man asked.

"There's someone there I want to talk to," José said.

He began to undress, and the fat man helped him with trembling hands. When José stood naked in front of him, the fat man looked at his legs and his thighs and began to cry again.

"Perhaps I shall go tomorrow morning," José said mockingly. "But give me those rings, both of them, the diamond and the ruby."

The fat man began taking off his rings. "You can have anything you want, but don't leave me."

"I'll leave you all right . . . tomorrow morning. I know you. You just don't have what it takes. I can still hear the crowd jeering. I still can feel the horns of the bull. You have no power."

The fat man took a handkerchief from his pocket and wiped his eyes. Then he shook his head.

"I don't understand you, boy," he said. "I don't know what's eating you. I bought you the best clothes, and when you had your fun with girls I never said a word. You can have everything you want from me. Tomorrow I will buy you a car—an American car. Please don't leave me."

"I don't need you," José said. "I'll find my own way."

He left the city in the morning, on a bus, and three days later he was back home again. The valleys were slowly drowning in darkness as he left the bus and the cypresses died slowly, still pointing the way. The bus stopped, leaving him alone in the dust, and he walked through the empty lanes; it was so different from all his dreams, the silent homecoming, empty-handed, and there was no hero's welcome, only a few barking dogs.

He was now eighteen and it had been three years since he left the village. He was hungry, but he did not go home, for there was an anger in him and a need to know, to find out. He walked toward the lake and looked at its last silver glow, with the boats shrouded in their nets, and on the distant island the enormous granite statue of the Liberator still standing, as on the day he was born. Beyond were the mountains and the old, overthrown gods with petals of wild flowers protecting their eyes; he had often helped his father to put fresh petals over their open eyes, so as to spare them the sight of the earth that had become so wicked since it had been taken away from them.

At the lake, he turned left and walked toward the house. It had aged and the reeds had grown bigger around it. The adobe walls had holes in them and they smelled of decay. He walked in, wondering if the old priest was still alive, and then he saw him sitting by the table, erect, silent, lost in thoughts. The table was covered with flowers and herbs, and José knew their message well. Green for fertility, red for good health, white against evil. Tomorrow morning, as on every day, they would be laid down in the church at the feet of the saint.

Father Chrisostomo looked at him but it was getting dark and he did not seem to recognize him. José stepped aside so that whatever light came through the door could hit his face, and the old man put his glasses on and stared at him.

"So you are back," he said. "The town did not eat you. Or perhaps you are running from the police? When our young men come back to the village, it is because they are in trouble. That's how it is."

"I just came back for a few days," José said. "I wanted to see you before you die, old man. It will be soon now. I wanted to talk to you again."

"I still have seven months left before I die," the old man said, with satisfaction.

"How do you know?"

"The new priest won't be here before that."

José sat down and looked at the old man. It was a very ancient face with deep crevices, and if it was dark as a

Cujon's face should be, the hair and beard were white and Spanish. Strange that Cujon hair never turns quite white, José thought.

"How was life in the city?"

"I've had some bad luck."

"Maybe you deserved it."

José looked at the green, red and white flowers and herbs on the table.

"Tell me, what is the worst sin?"

"They are all bad," the old man said. "There's nothing to choose. They all lead to hell."

"But which one is worst of all?"

"I don't know," the old man said wearily. "To kill your mother is about the worst, I should think. Sodomy is bad too. You just can't put your foot right in this world."

"But what's the sin that really gives you goose flesh, old man?"

"I am too old to get goose flesh. My skin is too hard."

"Is murder the worst?"

"Yes, murder is about the worst. Incest is very bad, too."

"What did you say? I don't know this word."

"Incest."

"What's that?"

"It is when a man and a woman of the same blood commit a mortal sin together."

"It is very bad? Is it the worst?"

"You go to hell for it," the old man said. "But why do you ask?"

"If somebody came to you and asked you what would please the devil most, what would you say?"

The old priest thought it over carefully. Then he shook his head.

"I don't know," he said. "Everything pleases him. Everything we do. He likes everything we do. He just stands there and watches us as we wallow in sin, and laughs happily."

"But still, there must be some things that please him more than others."

"Incest is bad," the old man said. "You go straight to hell for that. Incest marks you as the devil's own. But why do you ask me, boy? Did you come all the way back from the city just to ask me this?"

The boy sat silent for a moment, clasping his hands.

"Anyone could have told you."

"You are the only one I trust," the boy said. "You are a saint."

The old man looked at him sternly.

"This is blasphemy. I am a poor village priest, and that is all. You must pray for me when I die."

It was getting darker. The boy could see only the old man's shadow now and the white hair.

"Remember what you used to say?"

"No, I can hardly remember anything now. My old dog died only last week, and I don't even remember his name."

"Pedro," the boy said.

"Yes," the old man said, quickly. "Pedro. I am glad you remembered it."

"You used to say: the wicked shall inherit the earth."

"I remember that too," the priest said, "and that is what is happening. They burn the churches, they kill, they torture, it's the truth. You are a good boy. I remember you well, although I have forgotten your name. What is your name?"

"José. José Almayo."

"Yes, José. You went to the city."

"I came back."

"You see, I remember you, and yet they say that I can't

remember my prayers, and they sent for a new priest. I remember. You wanted to be a bullfighter."

"I tried," the boy said, "but I was no good. It was not given to me. I have no talent."

"You could be a good fisherman, like your father."

The boy got up.

"What was that word again?"

"What word? I said no word."

"The worst sin. The thing that makes the devil happy."

"You must not think so much about the devil. You must think about God."

"Good-by. Die in peace."

"Good-by. I am glad you have come."

Then he pulled out his gun. The priest was now only a shadow and as his eyes were bad, José knew that he would not see. He preferred it that way. But maybe that was the mistake, he had come to think since. Maybe that was why the whole thing failed, because of that moment of weakness when he did not want the old man to know that he was going to kill him.

He waited a few seconds with the gun in his hand and then took a good aim at the shadow and pulled the trigger. The old man sat still and erect as if nothing had happened, and perhaps nothing had happened after all. Perhaps nothing ever happened, nothing ever mattered, perhaps there was no such thing as sin, crime, and there was not even such a thing as evil.

He could feel drops of sweat on his temples as the thought hit him, for nothing scared him more than the idea that the earth belonged to men and that there was no hell, no heaven, no supreme talent, no outside help, only dust and nothingness.

He remembered how he stood there watching the old

man sit so quietly with the bullet in him; he did not fall at all. Maybe there was not enough of him left to fall down. He was not heavy enough. Only his hands and his head dropped limply, and that was all.

The boy remained a long time in the darkness, listening, waiting, but only the bells on the boats, as the wind raised some waves, tinkled among the reeds. He waited. He felt that he could hardly have done better and if ever he was to be given a place among the great of this evil world, this was the moment, this was his chance.

He looked around him and then it seemed to him that something moved suddenly, and a pair of eyes began to glitter, yellow and fiendish. A smile came to his lips, but the cat jumped and was gone, and he stood alone, facing the dead body, in an empty universe without talent or magic or power.

A night bird cried in the dark. The bells tinkled, the door groaned on its hinges. But nothing happened, nobody came in, no strange appearance, no fiery eyes, nobody came to say: "Well done, boy. You have really done your worst now. I am buying what you have to offer. In exchange, you will have the talent to be whatever you want and the power and the fame. You will be happy on this earth. Because the earth belongs to me, as the Heavens to God. I am the giver here."

The smile left his lips and he looked toward the door, though he knew that the devil did not need a door to enter. His faith and his hope were still intact. It was just not possible that men were alone and free, that they had no master.

Maybe it was that moment of weakness, of pity when he had not wanted the old man to see his gun, when he had waited deliberately for darkness before pulling it out, that had cost him his prize. Maybe this was interpreted as a sign that there was still some goodness left in him and that he was unworthy. But he was still very young, only eighteen. He would harden in time. He would know no mercy, no pity, in his search for power, for talent. He was still young enough to be a great bullfighter, the pride of his village, of his country. Or a great bandit. Or a politician, or a general. But he needed a little help. He needed talent.

He turned away from the body and looked out of the house and saw the lake where the moon was swimming as if trying to climb into a boat from the water. He glanced around but there was no one among the reeds, and the sky was riddled with stars. He wondered, briefly, desperately, if one had to pray to God for permission to meet the devil. Then he clenched his fists and began to shout obscenities at the sky, at the volcanoes which rose on the other side of the lake, with their ruins of temples and the dead faces of useless gods with petals of fresh flowers put over their eyes to protect them against the sight of the world.

When there was nothing left in him but hunger and thirst and the furious blood beating against his temples, he walked toward the village.

There was no police force there, no telephone, no electricity. It would take them three or four days to find the body, and then no one would care or bother to find out who did it and why. And then he could always lie and deny it, and as they all knew that the old man loved him, they would never believe that he had killed him.

X

HE STEPPED INTO the house, lowering his head, and hesitated a second, observing the dimly lit faces around the table. They had not changed much. His mother was in the corner, bent over the stove. She turned her head toward him and then looked away, as if he were a stranger, and no one said anything, except that his older brother showed his teeth in an ironic grin. Yet his clothes were good and clean and expensive and he looked rich. Or perhaps his brother had not noticed the two rings on his fingers—then he would not have grinned. His father's hair was still black. He glanced at the girl and saw that she had breasts now. His father stared at him, impassive and aloof, as if he did not believe the clothes and the rings, as if he did not believe that José was truly successful.

They did not even ask him to sit down, and then the mother suddenly came to the table with a new plate and pushed an empty box for him to sit on. He sat down. He waited a moment, but no one spoke and only the brother grinned again. José asked himself how much one could get for killing a brother, how high it rated, and if it would be a good mark for him. He felt pretty sure the devil would like that. He felt deeply offended, fumbled in his pocket and brought out a handful of bills. He pushed them toward his father, who went on eating his fish.

The old man looked at the money.

"They say you lead a bad life," he said.

"It's a good life," José said. "Look."

He showed his hands with the ruby and the diamond rings. They stared at them. His mother came up from the fire, and looked at her son's hands. The girl's eyes brightened and she smiled.

"Look, all of you," José said. "I am doing well for myself."

The brother was no longer smiling.

"And it's only the beginning," José said. "I can have all I want. Everything. I know the way."

"What do you do for a living?" his father asked.

"Nothing," José said. "You just have to have the right contacts, that's all. You meet important people and they introduce you to others and you climb higher and higher. It's like a totem pole, and there's someone very big waiting at the top. You get American cars and clean women and fine clothes like the ones I have, and rings."

He stretched out his hands again, spreading the fingers. The girl touched the ruby ring.

"It's beautiful."

José took it from his finger and handed it to her.

"Take it. Keep it."

The girl looked scared.

"They say you keep bad company," the father said, "that you are bad."

"Sure, I am bad," José said. "You have to be if you want to go places and meet the right people. I am going to be a great bullfighter, the greatest of them all."

The brother looked at him mockingly again.

"I saw you fight," he said.

José's body tensed. He could feel his heart pounding and he did not know what to say.

"I went to the city and saw you fight," his brother said.

"When?" José asked.

"Last month," his brother said. "It cost me all I had but I went to the town and saw you fight. I heard the crowd jeering and booing and laughing at you, and I was jeering and booing and laughing with them. It was worth it. You are bad. I never saw anyone quite so bad as you, and I have seen many."

The father went on eating. No one looked at him except the brother.

"One day I'll kill you," José said.

"Keep quiet," the father said.

"And perhaps I'll kill you too," José said. "All of you. I would do it for nothing. Yes, I am bad, but one day I will be good."

"You have no talent," the brother said.

"One day, I will come back to this village and I'll show you," José said.

"You have nothing to show," the brother said. "I saw you."

"You don't have to be a bullfighter," the father said, suddenly. "Why don't you try something else?"

"I will," the boy said. "One day I will come back here and there will be flags, and flowers, and my portrait every-where. And you will be honored because I am your son. I'll have all the power and everything it takes. I know how to get it. I know where it comes from. I have been to school and I know. You don't even know how to read. I can read. I was taught all there is to know and I know the answers. I know how people become presidents and generals, rich and powerful."

"Your mouth is still bigger than your ass, I see," the brother said. "And when I look at those rings I can see that your ass must be pretty big too."

"Enough," the father said.

José put his hand in his pocket. But no, he could not do it now. Not at his father's table, not in his house. Perhaps that was again a moment of weakness, but he could not do it like that. I still have to learn, he thought, I still have a long way to go. No wonder there is no sign, no answer. I am only a beginner. There are still things I cannot do. I am not bad enough yet. But one day I'll be bad enough. Then everything will be given to me.

He pushed his plate away and got up.

"I'll find my way to the top. I know how it's done." He walked out.

They did not believe him. They were stupid people who had never been to school and knew nothing about the world. He stood there watching the night and wondering where to sleep and how soon his luck would change. It was all much more difficult than he had thought. There was too much competition around. It was not enough just to be bad. One had to be the worst. Then he felt a hand on his shoulder and took the cigar out of his mouth. It was the girl.

"You forgot your ring."

"Keep it," he said. "I'll have many more for you, if you come with me."

"I know what you will ask me to do in the city," the girl said.

"Then stay here and rot."

"I'll come," she said. "I've had enough of fish."

He was a little disappointed later that night when he discovered that she was no longer a virgin, and when she told him that his brother had been doing it with her for she did not remember how long, he got almost scared and felt goose flesh.

So her brother had sinned with her for several years, and yet he was still a stinking fisherman, a mud worm, trembling

with fever at night. But Father Chrisostomo had told him
this was a mortal sin. There must be some merit in committing it; it should bring some sort of recognition, some
encouragement to persevere. Surely there was enough evil
in what his brother had committed to help him out of his
dirty fisherman's clothes, out of his filthy hole and into the
world. Surely it had given him the right to some sort of
reward.

"Why are you shivering?" the girl asked.

Maybe nothing you did with your body was truly bad, he
thought. Maybe the body was not important, you could not
use it as a key. Whatever you did with your body, it always
remained innocent and untouched. You could not find evil
there.

And then he remembered Father Sebastián, and his
warnings against the perils of the flesh. He felt a little better and more hopeful and drew her once more toward him.
Then he lit a cigar and thought for a moment. He knew
that he was too impatient. It probably took many years and
a lot of guts; one had to prove that one was really bad and
determined to be a great man, not just pretending. Then
one day, suddenly at a most unexpected moment, it would
come, it would come to you, and the world would be yours.
He was only a novillero now. He had yet to prove himself
truly worthy.

In the city, during the next few weeks, it all worked
very well. They posed for pictures and gave exhibitions for
tourists in the back of a café. The owner of the café was
always in search of new talent and he would speak for
hours in a dreamy, nasal voice about how difficult it was to
find it, and how little enthusiasm and fire and inspiration
there was in the average performer nowadays.

"You either have it in you or you don't," he would say,

sitting heavily on his stool. "If it is given to you and you burn with talent, then people leave the place feeling that they have seen something truly wicked, something really great, but it takes a real artist, not just anyone. You have it in you, boy. You will draw a lot of attention. The tourists will come to watch you. They like to see something truly wicked. It gives them hope."

XI

HE DID STRIKE UP a few acquaintances. Two or three local politicians asked them to their houses to perform for their friends. An American gangster on the run from New York had hired them for several days, but he was drunk all the time and they had had to steal his wallet and leave him without really getting anywhere. There were several rich men who gave them money and bothered them with their persistence, but they were just ordinary men, desperate, exhausted and often scared, men without power, even if they pretended to be this or that and looked important.

José got tired of the café, of his exhibitions, of the owner, of his promises that never came true.

"It's not easy to meet the right people, boy," he would say again and again, "but you will succeed. You are young and good-looking and you will make your way into the world. You have what it takes."

José was also tired of Rosita's gaiety and singing, and somehow he could not imagine that what they were doing was truly a sin. Whenever she had a moment, she would rush to church and pray, and he was sure that she was ruining whatever chances they had to meet anyone or get anywhere. She gave him the feeling that he was condemned to innocence. José understood why his brother was still a fisherman back there in the village: she was pure and you just could not do anything about it. About the time he was reaching this conclusion, she fell in love with a cab driver and married him.

She was now a fat woman with several children and she called them "my little angels," so nothing had come out of it.

He lived precariously, trying to seduce girls and then convince them to work for him, or standing in the streets in the hope of being picked up by some tourist, peddling dope for bigger dealers, who had even bigger dealers above them, who in turn were responsible to someone they did not know and spoke about only in hushed, awed tones, someone who was obviously at the top of the totem pole.

Then he began to act as a talent scout for strip tease joints, bordellos and blue film producers. But he was already disillusioned with sex. No matter how far one went in that direction, there was no evil there; it always remained commonplace and much too available. It did not open to you the door to any forbidden and secret land. One had to do much worse than that. He was thinking more and more of entering politics.

The old village priest, with his ideas of what the greatest sin was, had been wrong. In the modern world, the two sins which he had selected as tops, as the most likely to attract attention and bring recognition, sodomy and incest, were nothing at all. They did not get you far, not even in trouble with the law.

The true talent was elsewhere—in government, in the police, or in the army. There, if you really did your worst, you could become a dictator or a general and be given all the good things of life. He liked to muse in the little archives shop behind the Square of the Liberator; it was full of photographic documents of the last forty years of the country's history. The walls were covered with pictures of firing squads and hanged politicians and bandits and executed leaders who did not make good, and of those who had hanged their enemies first and so went on to become respected and famous, of all the great historical figures of the nation, taken as far back as photographic art went.

There was, particularly, one picture there, of a general shot for accepting bribes—he had probably omitted to share the money with his superiors—which always filled José with admiration and respect, as he looked at it. The general stood before the firing squad, smoking a cigarette in a long white holder, smiling and pointing his finger at his heart, to help the soldiers with their aim. He was completely calm and self-assured because, José told himself, he will knew everything he had done, all the thievery, the exactions, the protection given to those who could afford to pay him against those who could not, the ruthless persecutions, the jailing of peasants and students whenever there was a threat of revolt in the air—and so he could appear with a completely clear conscience before his master, who would receive him with open arms and then perhaps send him back to earth for another tour of duty, and make him an even bigger man, perhaps even a President, or an American monopolist, one of those who own the world, as the Communists assured everyone with such an impressive conviction. The generals always return. José thought respectfully.

He bought the picture of his hero and carried it always in his pocket, just for luck: it gave him a sense of personal physical contact, a feeling of being a little closer to the source of all power.

José continued for a while acting as talent scout for the blue circuit, but without illusions, just to make a living and to establish a few political contacts, as vice was still the best meeting ground for that purpose. It was the least you could do if you wanted to get anywhere. It was like getting a cheap membership card, accessible to all. You had to have it in your pocket just to have all the doors open to you, but it could not take you far.

He still peddled marijuana and heroin in the streets and everyone knew him as a thoroughly reliable fellow who would do anything. In his free moments, after dark, the thing he enjoyed most was to sit in one of the best night clubs of the capital and watch the performance.

It was thus that one night he had come across the Great Maestro at the El Señor, a place run by a former café owner from the blue circuit whom José had been supplying with acts and who had made good.

The Great Maestro was an Italian. He was a robust man with a black beard that was held down by a crooked smile, with brushy eyebrows, a strong curved nose, black-dyed hair that was getting a little sparse in the middle but was long and crinkly and stood on end at both sides of the head, giving it a strangely electric appearance. There was no question that he was the most talented man José had ever seen. It was not only that he could summon flying doves from nowhere, and that personal objects which the audience felt sure were in their pockets would be suddenly found at the bottom of his top hat; it was not only that with one snap of his fingers he would summon a lit cigar from the air, then with another snap a flask of brandy, then a glass, and then, while drinking the brandy and smoking the cigar, he would suddenly snap his fingers again and everything would be gone, vanished. All that was already admirable, but he could do more.

One night, as José sat at the bar with a few friends, watching the act, the Great Maestro noticed his fascinated attention and asked him to come onto the floor. Then he turned toward the audience:

"Ladies and gentlemen, each of us carries in his heart

a secret longing, a dream. . . . Take this young man, for instance. I have never seen him before, but I like him. I am going to do something for him. Ladies and gentlemen, I request your complete attention. It gives me great pleasure to perform before you an act of unparalleled difficulty, entirely without precedent in the whole history of magic—I must ask you for total concentration and silence. . . . In a few seconds, this young man is going to see his most secret dream come true, and he is going to tell us everything about it."

He looked deep into José's eyes and moved his fingers before them a few times. José's face was very white. He stood there completely stiff, breathing heavily, and then his eyes widened . . .

"That's right," the magician said. "You are seeing it now. . . . Tell us, my friend, what you see . . ."

"El Señor!" José shouted. "El Señor!"

And it was exactly as in Father Chrisostomo's description of the evil one, or in the pictures of him he had seen so often in the Communist press. There were flames around him, but also mountains of gold with figures in American dollars written on each pile, naked, wriggling couples in the background, like on the blue circuit, only much more beautiful. And El Señor had cloven feet and horns, just as the priests had always told him, except that he was wearing a very good suit of Italian silk, and he was offering dollars and smoking a big cigar, like a rich gringo tourist. . . . The audience roared with laughter at the superstitious young Indian who was describing his naïve idea of the devil to them in an excited voice and who, when the magician woke him from his trance, stared at him in awe: it was obvious that he had been badly shaken and that he had never heard of hypnotists before.

The next evening, José was back at the night club, but the Great Maestro did not pay the slightest attention to him. He chose someone else in the audience, an American tourist with a fat behind and sweaty face, who was made to see a lot of naked girls and that was all. José left before the act was over and went to the Hotel Cortés, where the magician was staying. He took the key and went up to his room.

It was late when the Great Maestro came in, and José saw at once that he was drunk. The Italian looked at the young hoodlum in the immaculate blue suit, with the white panama hat, blue shirt and white tie, sitting in a chair.

"What are you doing here?" he asked in a thick, drunken voice.

José felt bewildered: that a man with such powers and with such contacts would need to get drunk was something he could not understand.

"Why didn't you call me up tonight?" he asked. "Why didn't you make me see again?"

The Italian had taken off his coat. He was in tails and above the white waistcoat his black beard and face looked even darker.

"Why should I?" he said. "I choose another subject each evening. Otherwise, the public would think I do my act with a stooge. I don't need stooges. I don't need you. Get out."

He sat down in a chair and began to take off his shoes.

"I can do it with anyone. I have the power . . ."

He looked cunningly at the young Indian and winked.

"A supernatural power, you understand. It has been given to me."

José swallowed hard. His face became a little paler and his nostrils narrowed. His heart was pounding.

"I am the greatest of them all," the Great Maestro said.

"I open in Las Vegas next week. There's no one to match me. Give me an audience of twenty thousand and with one snap of my fingers I make them see what I want them to see. There's the German, Hans Kruger, and the Frenchman, Belladon, but I tell you they have a long way to go before they can match my act. I have performed before kings and before great dictators, before truly important people. I have all the medals."

He belched.

"I don't know why I came to this dirty hole. Not for money, certainly. As a matter of fact, I know why—girls. They have the youngest here and they show you things you can't see elsewhere. They're completely corrupt here, completely rotten, that's what I like. I had a little number yesterday, and what she did is nobody's business, she was truly talented, she really had it in her. I just love the place. The blue films—they show them here to you in the open theaters and you even have kids in the audience. Just great! Anything goes. The act in the night club is only an excuse. I come here to have a good time. Say, boy, if you know any special act that I haven't seen yet, something truly filthy, mind you, because I've seen everything—not just the old stuff with the donkey, they do it everywhere—now, do you know of anything new, boy? Something truly new?"

He was begging now, almost imploring, and his face was strangely worried, anxious.

"Make me see again," José asked quietly.

The Great Maestro yawned.

"Not tonight. I am tired. Some other time. Now, perhaps, if you know some willing, naughty little girls . . . something different. They say that there is a new act somewhere in this town that's truly formidable. But I wonder. . . . There is a limit to what you can do with sex. I am a great amateur of pornography, but they all do the same thing. I have seen it all in Bangkok, Burma, in Japan. Very limited. Ask me some other time, young man."

He yawned and then his eyes widened and his mouth opened as he found himself staring into the muzzle of a gun.

"Come on," José said, through his teeth. "I mean it. Make me see him again: I want to talk to him."

"To whom?" the badly frightened magician stammered. "What did I show you last night? I don't . . ."

Then he remembered. He tried not to laugh. A quick, cunning smirk was all he permitted himself. One had to be careful with those primitive Indians. Their pagan gods had been taken away from them, the new God had never answered their prayers, and yet the deep, aching craving for the supernatural was still in them, and made them the best, the most gullible audience in the world.

"All right, young man, you have won. Just relax now. I can't show you anything, if you remain tense. And put that gun away. I can't do much when I'm scared."

José stuck his gun under his belt. The magician got up from the chair. He looked deep into the boy's eyes and made a few passes with his hands. José found himself slowly drifting away, and he felt a mounting emptiness, as if he were taking leave of his mind, of his heart, of the whole world. The next thing he knew was a pain in his ribs, a deep, violent ache. Then he felt a pain in his head, and his whole body, as it returned to him, was one mass of pulsating wounds. He was lying face down in the gutter, in the street behind the hotel. The Great Maestro had put him to sleep and then he had called for help; they had beaten him and thrown him out.

He sat still for a while, his head lowered, looking at his soiled clothes. He didn't mind the pain: that has always been a part of being an Indian. The only thing that mattered was that the magician had cheated him. Or perhaps he had been put to a test, to see how determined he was. It took him only three days to catch up with the Great Maestro again: he knew where to look for him. He went through the old joints behind the Liberator's Square, and through those in the Calle Chávez, and the two or three other small streets next to it, where even the politicians in office did not like to be seen; when some truly new and depraved act was performing there, they summoned the performers to their palaces, for respectability's sake.

José did not do the rounds alone this time. He took two friends with him. One was Pepe, who could break a man's neck with a snap of his fingers, but who had given it up long ago, because he didn't believe in anything anymore, he had lost faith. But the second one, Arzaro, was still ambitious and determined to get on in life. He had been the President's bodyguard at a time when the latter was only a small-time politician just strong enough to give his protection to a few local businessmen.

They found the Great Maestro on the third night, at the back of a café where a few gringos watched an animal act. The act was strictly routine, and José felt a moment of doubt and bewilderment. Why a man with such powers would pay to see these cheap tricks was a mystery to him.

The Great Maestro recognized them at once and his face turned green. They did not have to pretend, not in this joint. They were known there and respected, and their names already meant something. They just gestured to the Italian to get up and to follow them, and he did.

There were a few rooms available on the premises, where the most daring of the gringos sometimes went with a girl, or had private showings. They took him there. They didn't beat him up. They didn't have to. The Great Maestro had taken one look at them and that was enough. Pepe surely had the biggest hands in the land, and Arzaro was so loaded with heroin that his pupils were gone.

"Don't frighten me," the magician said, in a quivering voice. "Don't touch me, or I won't be able to do a thing for you." His face took on a self-assured, cocky look. He knew these superstitious, uneducated Indians; he knew how deeply his hypnotic powers impressed their simple minds. They often waited at the door of the theater to touch him for luck, begging him to cure them, to make them rich, to give them children. He loved it. Those were moments when he almost believed in himself.

José stepped forward.

"Make me see him again," he said.

The magician quickly repressed a grin.

All right, I'm going to make you see him, you hoodlum, he thought. There were not many hypnotists who could do that. In fact, he knew only of the German, Kruger, who was said to be able to perform the same trick. Usually, even the best of them had to use their voices and suggest aloud what they wanted the subject to see, but he did not have to do it. He did not have to use his voice at all. He just let the subjects follow their own imagination.

"Here he is," he said. "Talk to him. Tell him why you asked to see him."

He stepped back and watched. The Indian stood there with clenched fists, his body rigid, his eyes closed, his head thrown back, and his face dark and eager. What he said carried in it the bitterness of centuries, and the whole history of his people, of their hopelessness and wretchedness, was behind his words. Without knowing it, he was making his first political speech, and expressing more clearly the rancor of the peasants who had never known any hope than all those who spoke the language of statistics, who denounced the lack of schools, the lowest standard of living in the world, the arrogant wealth of the few and the dark ignorance of the masses.

"My name is José Almayo," he said in a quick, staccato voice. "Perhaps you have heard of me. I've done everything I knew to please you, because that is the only way. I'll do more. I'll learn. But you must help me. I'm only an Indian. I need all your help to get to the top. It has never been done before. The government, the army, the police have always taken care of that. You've always given them your help, because they deserve it: they are cruel and wicked. The people are good, and they work hard—but it's not their fault—they don't know any better. They are only peasants. But I know. I've seen the world. I've understood. I know what it takes. I'm willing."

Pepe and Arzaro were staring at him, trembling with fear. The Great Maestro himself felt a little put out. He took a toothpick from his vest pocket and began to chew it, watching uneasily the massive, powerful figure with clenched fists and granite-like face raised almost menacingly toward the sky. He had traveled widely and he knew that millions of Indians were thus raising their eyes, clenching their fists and waiting, all over the South American continent. If only it occurred to them to put their fists together, they could shake the world. Fortunately, they did not know where the true power lay—they were too ignorant and too superstitious, just like this peasant who was trying to strike a bargain with the devil—the creation of his own primitive mind—trying to sell him his soul.

Have you ever thought what your little crummy soul is worth, anyway? the Great Maestro thought. You poor skunk, there is no one to buy it from you. It's the cheapest commodity on the market and you can't get anything for it. You're stuck with it.

When José emerged from his trance, the magician was gone. Pepe was gaping at him and sweating profusely and Arzaro was so scared that he had pulled out his knife.

"Where is he? Why did you let him go?"

José left the place and went straight to the El Señor, but the magician did not appear. He had left town that very night, heading for the United States. His engagement at the night club wasn't quite over, but he was not taking any chances. For a long time he remembered the strange young Indian standing there with an expression of somber determination on his face and somehow he felt that he would not care to meet him again.

The Great Maestro had left such a profound impression on José's mind that he gave up the blue circuit completely and became a talent scout for the legitimate night clubs and music halls, in some vague, confused hope of another contact. Almost every night he dreamt of magic: there was no other way for a Cujon Indian to rise above his squalid, centuries-old fate of hopelessness and neglect. Dark veiled figures in tails and silk top hats leaned over his bed, looking into his soul to see if it was wicked and cruel enough to be permitted to take his place among the great of this world, if he truly had it in him. He was still peddling drugs and now had five girls working for him, but that was hardly enough, there was a lot of competition, things were difficult for a beginner, and he knew that he had to do a lot more if he were to prove himself worthy. He continued to visit the little shop of historical archives behind the Liberator's Square, studying with his serious, respectful eyes the pictures of all the great national figures, politicians, generals, rich, powerful men of past and present, famous for their ruthlessness and wickedness, who had succeeded in striking a bargain and had made good.

He paid a great deal of attention to the anti-American propaganda that was sweeping the land, and was becoming more and more impressed with America. He always stopped to listen when political agitators in the markets explained to the Indians how childish and ignorant it was to believe that the evil one had cloven feet and horns: no, he was driving a Cadillac, smoking a cigar, he was a big American businessman and imperialist who owned the land they were toiling on and was always trying to buy the people's soul and conscience with his dollars. It struck him very much; he began to look at American tourists with new respect.

He was now beginning to command some attention and esteem. The police were friendly; he was obviously a young man going places. They all knew that it was only a matter of time before he would enter politics. He was not rich yet and he couldn't pay them, but he was useful and willing to stick his neck out whenever a man in high position needed what was known as "left-hand help." He had made valuable contacts during his years on the blue circuit and he was on familiar terms with influential people who now often let him in on some of their business ventures. He knew already almost everyone worth knowing in the present regime. But the regime was at the end of its tether, with all the people in the right places already rich and fat and beginning to take themselves seriously, building roads, schools, and even talking about cleaning up the capital, so as to ruin things for the others. It was high time for a change.

New political parties were emerging everywhere, immediately suppressed by the government and then going underground and becoming secret "action groups." José belonged to them all; he was determined to pick the winner. The Army was not committed, but the six or seven generals at the top had been sitting there for a long time, and the colonels were getting impatient. But no one knew yet in which direction to jump. They were all anti-American, of course, and anti-Communist, although they all claimed some sort of Socialist trend to attract the masses. To be anti-American for a politician meant to play hard to get, so that, once they were in power, they could dictate their terms to the American firms.

José was soon able to take over the El Señor night club, the best place in town, and he had talent scouts now who were looking for new acts for him.

He also had an American girl friend.

XII

SHE HAD STAGGERED into the night club one evening, sobbing, disheveled and badly frightened. He had picked up a little English by then from his dealings with the tourists, and he managed to make some sense out of what she cried out, hysterically. She had been riding in a taxi to some tourist attraction on the outskirts of the city—the ruins of a temple where they used to have human sacrifices—and the driver had taken her into an alley and then had raped her and snatched her bag from her.

There was nothing unusual in her story. José had often done this himself, as he later admitted to her, when he was a beginner, starving both for cash and women.

But the American girl took it all rather badly, talking all the time about a grandmother she had back in Iowa and about the degree in languages she had taken at some university, and sobbing hysterically. Obviously she felt that the taxi driver should not have raped her, of all people, but someone else who did not have a grandmother and a university degree.

The bartender had been to the States and as José listened carefully, smoking a cigar, he expressed the opinion that the girl had probably been a virgin. It often happened out there. None of it made much sense to José, but he did grasp that the girl had a good education and that she was from a respectable family. Somehow, that made her sexually more attractive to him. She was a good-looking girl, with very white skin, a very ripe mouth and a little, upturned nose.

But the hair was bad. She cut it very short, so there was not enough of it. He liked very long hair that filled one's hand.

At first, she wanted him to call the police, but soon gave up the idea when he told her that it would then get into the papers and then, the bartender explained, with a quick wink to José, the American papers would pick it up and her grandmother would find out.

She was alone in town, a tourist, and she spoke very little Spanish—that's why she had come here, in the first place, to perfect her Spanish and to broaden her cultural horizon —and then, on her first day . . . She began to sob again. He gave her a drink, and another, and took her to dinner; it was good for him to be seen with an American girl. America was a big, mighty country, and he felt suddenly, irresistibly attracted to the girl.

She had too much to drink and she looked at José as if he were a savior. She was speaking to him in her bad Spanish, and he was trying his bad English on her. She hardly knew what she was doing when he took her later to his apartment above the night club. When he began to undress her, she tried to argue again.

"You do this because you despise me," she said. "Please be nice to me, please. I am lonely, and I need someone to protect me. I have only my grandmother in the world. . . ."

She was still mumbling something about her grand-mother when he took her, and she went to sleep before he had finished. The next morning, when she saw José, who was lying naked next to her, she began to sob again.

"I am a nymphomaniac," she cried. "I am ab-so-lute-ly destroying myself!"

José saw clearly that she was an educated girl because she used words he had never heard before. Now that she was no longer drunk, she looked at him reproachfully.

"You shouldn't have done that."

"Why? It was okay," he said.

"Well, I think you are nice, anyway. You have such a beautiful, noble forehead and extraordinary eyes. Are you Spanish?"

"Yes."

"Do you want me to go away now?"

"You can stay."

She stayed. She stayed a week, then two, then two months. She often asked herself what made her stay, then what had attracted her to him in the first place. Even now, looking back on it all, she could not quite explain it. But then, there was one thing, she told Dr. Horwat later, looking straight into his eyes: it was not only physical. Of course, they were madly in love and it was such a new discovery to her, she had never had any previous experiences. The first few weeks, she lived in a sort of haze, and it was such a beautiful country, although so terribly poor. She just fell in love with the people—that was it.

Then, slowly, she began to realize that José was a very confused boy, that he had problems. He was terribly insecure and seemed to be driven by some inner anxiety, some profound frustration—she tried to find out a little about his childhood, but there was nothing he could tell, except extreme poverty—but as she held him in her arms and looked at his beautiful and always a little somber face, she knew that what he needed above all was sympathy, compassion and love.

When she tried to explain to José what psychoanalysis was, he seemed very interested: it sounded like talent all right, he told her. He asked her if he could book one of those fellows for his night club. He was very naïve and, she had to admit, completely uneducated. She suddenly saw a truly exciting possibility, a purpose: he needed her. She could help him. She was not going to turn didactic and annoying, or lecture him, but she did her best to cope with some of his ignorance, to give him at least a glimpse of the better things life had to offer.

She soon began to notice that the night club was not his only occupation, that he had strange friends, and she began to hear rumors about his criminal associations. It was evident that he was going through a bad and dangerous period in his life, and he had met her just in time. He had never been taught to believe in anything positive and constructive, and he had to learn it all the hard way. In a sense, he was a victim of colonialism, of centuries of exploitation. Her blood boiled with indignation when she began to know the country better, and to notice the poverty, the squalor, the lack of hope. It was only natural that a man like José should have fought his way out of poverty by certain means that would appear unacceptable back home. It was not his fault, he had been driven to it. She felt strongly that America should have done more for this country.

José never quite understood what she was trying to explain, but there was a struggling quality about her, the feeling of a captive bird beating its wings against a window-pane, that excited him. Besides, she was an American and everybody saw them together, and it was good for his reputation. He admired America. The Communists said that the Americans were evil, that they wanted to be masters of the whole world and that their tourists corrupted the land; according to them, everything that was aggressive, powerful, rich, corrupt and evil was in America, and although José expected that they were probably exaggerating, he was nevertheless impressed by their propaganda and tremendously attracted to the United States. Even the Catholic priests often said that the Americans got rich and powerful because they were selling their souls to the devil, and so he was beginning to listen to everything that came from the United States with respect, although he never admitted it—it was bad politics to be pro-America.

She soon discovered with delight that José had political ambitions; he was constantly entertaining prominent figures lavishly, and also helping generously with money, paying the young officers and civil servants and offering expensive presents to their wives. She had always wanted to do something creative and she had even taken a course in creative writing at the University of Iowa, but she didn't seem to have any real talent in that direction even though she had won a poetry contest once, in her high school days, so she had taken up painting and ceramics instead, without much result. But now, at last, she had a chance to do something truly constructive and wonderful, helping José to accom-plish great things, bring progress and democracy to this unhappy land. She lay awake at night, worrying, wishing she had taken a degree in social science; she would have felt less insecure, better prepared for her task.

"I have been fortunate enough to meet a man who is determined to dedicate himself to the welfare of his country," she wrote home. "He needs my help and it is an exciting, creative opportunity. I plan to remain here for some time."

She was terribly moved and upset when she realized how completely uneducated the poor boy was, although he had an excellent mind and a great curiosity, and was, in many ways, absolutely brilliant; it was just that the educational system in the country was so backward, at least one hundred years behind the times, and he had never had a chance. She wrote an angry letter to a girl friend, who was working as secretary to a Congressman from Iowa, stressing the urgency of American aid to the country through the establishment of a proper educational system and cultural assistance. The United Nations should have definitely done something about it. She mentioned the United Nations to José and discovered that he was quite well informed on the subject; one of his best friends represented the country there, and he was given diplomatic immunity, which meant that he didn't have to go through customs. José admired the organization very much. He thought that it could be very useful.

She made a visit to the American Embassy and told them that she wanted to know what, exactly, the United States was doing to help this country. They gave her some papers to read, and she discovered that American aid to the nation amounted to a very considerable sum each year, although where it all went was a complete mystery to her: the country had the worst telephone system imaginable, no public library, no decent university, the ministry of education was completely inactive, and there was not even an art museum—nothing, none of those elementary things absolutely essential to democratic progress.

She began to order books from home, hundreds of them —José had made her a very large allowance, and although she had been very reluctant to accept it at first, she relented in the end, for she felt she was acting as a sort of cultural adviser to him, so there was nothing wrong in it. She sat late at night, trying to condense the books she considered essential to a few clear sentences in Spanish, although José was quickly learning English—it was truly amazing. Actually she herself worked mostly from digests of great works, often already reduced to a few pages, there was so little time, and so much for him to learn

His apartment above the night club now had shelves of books along the walls, and she had specially bound copies of the American Declaration of Independence, of the American Constitution, and of Barclay's life of Lincoln prominently displayed on his desk.

She took great care, of course, to refrain from boring him or from trying to teach him too openly. She thought it would be fatal to their relationship, and that if he suddenly became too clearly aware of her intellectual and cultural superiority, he would be very hurt, his Latin pride would probably not tolerate this and she might easily lose him.

"They are so completely different from our men back home," she wrote to her girl friend. "They are very Spanish, in the old-fashioned, ridiculous way, and they like to feel that their women are inferior to them and submissive and, although I do not intend to give in, of course, it would be completely wrong to meet this sort of thing head-on. There are a lot of things I intend to change in José's character and outlook, but it has to be done progressively. It is a matter of mutual adjustment and of mutual respect."

She took great care never to lecture him and just dropped a few words here and there, in the hope that it would leave a mark. It did often seem, however, that she merely amused him, and then she felt hurt. There was an extraordinary assurance in him, a sort of total self-confidence, as if he knew everything there was to know about life and about the world. It was a good thing, of course, that he should believe in himself—self-confidence is essential in leadership —but in a way it was pathetic and touched her deeply and made her feel almost maternal; it was all based on such misconception and such ignorance, and even on superstition. One day, as they were driving to a party given by one of the generals, she tried to explain to him a few things about Buddhism, about detachment and contemplation.

He listened attentively, and then said: "Philosophy. Sure I know what it is. The priests have taught me. The earth is bad, money is evil, fornication is evil, everything good is bad. So what? So if a man wants to get to the top and have all those things, he's just got to be pretty bad himself. He has to make the right connections and prove himself reliable and worthy. Okay?"

She was quite shaken. It was really terrible to see how pessimistic he was. Of course, he was of very humble origin and had known terrible poverty and social inequities, and had to struggle so hard—and it had left a mark. He had seen too much evil around him, and so he was a little bitter. She did try to argue this philosophical point passionately, to tell him something of the beautiful things of life, but lately she had been drinking too much and somehow it all got lost in her mind and she just said: "Oh, my darling, you do have such a lot of wrong notions. I feel terribly, terribly guilty. We didn't do enough for this country. And of course all those centuries of colonialism—it has been all such an injustice."

And he loved her truly—that was the only thing that she felt certain about, although in many ways he still remained for her a mystery. She often wished she had a close friend here, whom she could trust completely, to whom she could confide the extraordinary moments of happiness she experienced with him, the feeling of total achievement, after one of his violent and endless embraces. Only a man who loved deeply and truly could give himself so completely to a woman. But those were things that one had to keep to oneself. She merely wrote to her girl friend: "He loves me passionately and quite touchingly, and never misses an opportunity to give me some new and wonderful proof of that."

His political future was beginning to look very promising; there were constant meetings in the back of the club and he had friends in all the different political factions in the country. There was a tremendous magnetism in him; it was something in the gray-green beauty of his eyes, in the firmness of the mouth and of the chin, that even carried a certain mark of ruthlessness: he was a born leader. Sometimes, as she watched him tenderly, she discerned a striking resemblance between his face and that of Abraham Lincoln. The eyes were different, of course, and the features were very Spanish—he had some Indian blood in him too, and he was quite rightly very proud of it—and he had no beard, but then there was something unmistakable—she didn't know quite what, or perhaps it was just that she had such confidence in everything he was going to do for this country.

She knew that it was being said in the capital that his night club was the center of every imaginable traffic and even vice. On several occasions, she did notice that he was procuring girls for some of his political friends and for some officers. She tried to take up this point with him, without actually accusing him of anything, and without making an issue of it, but he shrugged his shoulders and said: "It takes what it takes. How do you say that in America? Politics is dirty business, eh?"

The narcotics trade had been going on in the country for ages, and it was true that if drastic measures were taken against it, it would ruin a lot of people, and the whole economy of the country would be thrown off balance. One of the high police officials, José's friend, explained it all to her carefully, adding that any lowering of the country's standards of living and an economic slump would merely benefit the Communists, and Communism was a drug much more dangerous than heroin.

Then he added: "Our people are very poor. There are still very few opportunities offered to them, because we have never been helped by the big powers, we have always been exploited. In the valleys, the peasants have been chewing mastala leaves for centuries. It gives them a considerable amount of well-being and happiness, and one cannot just take it away from them without giving them anything else."

She knew that this was true, in a way, although the morality of the point was highly debatable. But then, she had come to accept that there was a very different kind of morality here, that this country was not like America at all, and that many things had to be approached here from a different point of view; it was often indispensable to change one's way of thinking and to make certain psychological adjustments. She felt confident that when José reached his full political stature, she would be able to exercise over him a salutary influence for the benefit of the country, and that he would then need her advice and listen to it more than ever. It was only a matter of timing. It would mean political suicide for him to come out openly now against certain social evils that were unfortunately almost traditional here. One day they would clean up the country together. There was absolutely no question that he adored her. He literally showered her with expensive presents, jewels, cars, clothes. She never would have dreamt of accepting this situation in America, of course, but then she was aware that they lived very differently here, that they had completely different standards of morality, and one just had to overcome one's personal prejudices and biases.

José had bitter and powerful enemies; several times there had been shooting at his night club and it was obvious that his life was in constant danger. But he dismissed her pleadings and explained to her calmly, in his newly acquired English, "I am going to make it. I have it in me, that's all. I have what it takes. They can shoot at me as much as they like, but the bullets, they're not for me. They just make a noise past my ears. I've got protection. The best there is— the very best!"

He believed in his star with a total assurance and she admired him and respected him for that.

He loved her deeply and was very proud of her, and of their relationship. He never showed his affection and his tenderness openly, because in many ways, psychologically speaking, these big, virile Latin men were like little boys, ashamed to show their feelings. He never allowed himself any display of emotion. She did wish she could find a way to help him there too; it was wrong to control one's feelings to such a point; he needed a total abandon, a total emotional release. A good psychotherapist would have dealt with this problem easily. Basically there was absolutely nothing wrong with him: it was just that he was a little inhibited. She knew she made him very happy, she was convinced that he was more attached to her emotionally and intellectually than physically and, in a way, this was only confirmed by the fact that she soon found out that he had other women. She did feel hurt a little, but she knew that the depth and the quality of their relationship was much deeper than anything sex could give, and the fact that he had other women merely proved that he was putting her in a completely different and infinitely higher category.

She did wish, however, that he did not go around with other women so openly; but then, one had constantly to remind oneself that this was not the United States, and he was not an American male, it was part of their morality here to have mistresses; and then—she didn't consider herself as his mistress at all.

XIII

HE HAD RENTED her a big house with six servants, which was very nice, although she didn't see him as often as before; he also had another girl living with him quite openly, and she tried to make friends with her. It was one of his usual passing affairs and one had to be civilized about this sort of thing, even though it was a little humiliating, in a superficial sort of way. They had a wonderful, creative relationship together, and it was wrong to reduce everything to a physical level: and then, she had always wanted to do something truly worth while, to build something beautiful, and this was her great opportunity.

She had already been quite successful in making José a better man. For instance, he could speak English fluently now. And whenever she went to the night club, they always gave her the best table and treated her as if she were already his wife. But it was only normal that they should live separately, and see each other more discreetly, because José was in the process of becoming the most influential man in the country and, of course, the best political platform was anti-Americanism. It wouldn't be too good for his political standing and for his reputation if he lived with an American girl too openly.

There were, of course, some moments of weakness, and even of panic. Probably because of the altitude and of all those black volcanoes towering around her, she often felt strangely oppressed and even panicky, and at times she could not think clearly at all. She knew that she should go home for a rest, but then, she couldn't leave José alone, just when he needed her most. Sometimes, she would look around her and find herself lying on the sofa in a strange house, in a strange land, where she had come two years ago only for a short visit, and then she would get frightened and begin to cry. But after she had a few more drinks, she would feel a little better. She knew the American Vice Consul's wife and often felt an urge to telephone her and beg her to let her stay with them, and then perhaps send her away, help her to go home. But she was aware that this was only a neurotic impulse and she always managed to resist it. She couldn't be such a failure. What she needed was something active to do, something constructive. She was so eager to help this country, and while waiting for greater things to come, there must still be something useful she could do. She decided to teach English in a school, and José, as usual, was very nice about it and very helpful. Every morning her black Cadillac would take her to a miserable little building beyond the market—one day she was going to see to it that there were proper schools built in this country everywhere—and then the chauffeur would open the door respectfully, his cap in his hand, and she would step out, sometimes a little drunk, and they would receive her respectfully. The teacher in charge was a very nice old man, and he would lead her into the classroom and the children were so sweet and attentive and looked with their big eyes at the beautifully dressed lady who was standing a little unsteadily by the blackboard writing strange words in a foreign language on it.

She never missed a class and her Spanish improved considerably; soon she could speak to the children fluently in their own language, and make friends with them. One day, when she was teaching class—the Spanish language fascinated her and she was learning very quickly, and could now speak without an accent, almost like a native—she felt a little hand in hers and she saw a little girl staring at her.

"Please don't cry," the girl said. "Why do you cry? I love you."

Then she realized that she had been sitting at her desk crying for God knows how long, and she hadn't even known it. She was getting neurotic. It had to stop. She was not going to be licked, and so she managed to do something she had no longer quite expected to have the courage to do: she managed to kick the habit.

She looked at the evangelist with a triumphant smile, and waited.

"The habit?" young Dr. Horwat repeated.

Well, yes. She didn't quite know herself how it all began. She had always resented bitterly the open heroin peddling that went on in the club—behind José's back of course—but it was impossible to prevent it. Almost everyone she knew was using the stuff, and actually it didn't seem to do them too much harm. Perhaps the evil effects of the drug had been exaggerated back in the States; they were such puritans there. One evening, someone suggested that she should try it herself; just to see what it was all about, before condemning it, and she soon found out that it helped a lot and didn't seem to have any bad effects, which just went to prove that one must reject all preconceived notions and never take anything for granted. She was tremendously happy and excited. She wrote to her grandmother that it was only a matter of weeks now before her fiancé would be a famous political leader, whose name would be known all over the world, and she was marvelously thrilled in discovering every day how beautiful and rich life could be, how many extraordinary and heavenly treasures it carried in its wonderful stream, and how many lies were spread by certain bigots about certain things that were a blessing to every human being.

She couldn't understand why people in the States had been so ridiculous about the drug and its bad effects—it had to be taken discriminately, that's all—and of course, she was in a privileged position because she always had a free supply of it. But then she did manage to stop it—just in time, too. She didn't quite know how she had found the strength to do it; it was something that was in the little girl's eyes when she had looked at her: it had somehow reminded her of herself. So she managed to shake off the habit.

Once more she gave the young evangelist one of her triumphant smiles, and waited.

Young Dr. Horwat opened his mouth to say something, but all he had to say was already in the horrified expression on his pale and haggard face. As the car jumped from stone to stone and kept him bouncing from the Cuban monster to the wretched girl, who for the last half-hour had been pounding him with one horror after another, he felt that he was riding through hell. Her story had upset him so much that he had almost forgotten the mortal peril that hung over their heads, for it was quite clear, by now, that they were being taken to some remote spot, far away from the main road, for their execution.

"My dear child," he exclaimed at last. "How could you . . . ?"

He was going to say "How could you sink so low?" but checked himself, and said merely: "How could you stay with such a man?"

"Oh, but you don't understand," she said. "It was not

only that I loved him and wanted to help. I still do, as a matter of fact—and I still feel that I can help him. But it was such an opportunity, you see, to do something truly creative, constructive, not only for him, but for this country. I, myself, come from pioneer stock—I suppose that's what it is, really. We Americans like to get things done, to build something. It's such a challenge to me, both the man and the country, and in a way, I have succeeded—not entirely, of course, but partially, and there is still time, as I'm still very young. And I am basically very strong and very stubborn."

Dr. Horwat took a good look at her. It was true that there was a certain defiant, almost aggressive stubbornness in her features. The mouth was very soft—he permitted himself to look at it twice—but the slightly upturned nose, the chin, the eyes did combine into an air of almost reckless determination.

But it was really José, she continued, more than anything or anyone else who had helped her to pull herself together. He had been visiting her regularly then, at least twice a month, and one day, as he sat there in his chair, staring at her with those wonderful eyes of his, she heard him say: "You mustn't come every night to the club. It is a big place now. The best in town. I am an important man, and you always get drunk and then you shriek. Last night you went completely crazy."

Her eyes widened.

"Did I? Did I, really?"

"And you take too much of the stuff," he said. "Perhaps you had better see a doctor. Or perhaps you would like to go home. Back to the States, eh?"

She suddenly had an awful feeling that he was trying to get rid of her. He had been acting rather strangely with her of late; it was as if he were secretly scared of her.

"No," she said stubbornly. "I don't want to go back home."

"Why?"

"I refuse to go. I refuse ab-so-lute-ly."

"It's okay," he said. "Just take it easy."

"I cannot leave you right now. You still need me. All those things we can do together . . . I haven't yet even begun, really—music, literature, painting. Darling José, I'm not trying to say that you are uneducated or primitive or anything of the kind, but I do mean that there are certain things you don't appreciate yet, simply because you don't know about them. You must read, darling, you simply must. It will open a new world for you. When you are in the government we'll do wonderful things together. We'll have a symphony orchestra here, and a public library, and everything. I can't go back home yet. I do know I haven't done much for you, but it took me so much time to adjust myself—it's such a new, and in many ways such a strange, environment. God, I feel I've failed you badly."

She began to cry. He was still staring at her in silence, in that strange, immobile way of his. But it was then that she noticed something in the expression on his face, something she had never noticed before: he looked scared. He looked either respectful or scared and, of course, she didn't understand why, not then anyway. He was such a strange man and she didn't quite realize how superstitious he was.

"Okay," he said. "Okay."

But she did see that she had to get a stronger grip on herself if she still wanted to be useful to him, if she wanted to have things done—she had big plans for this country and she just couldn't afford to let herself go to pieces. So she kicked the habit, simply because it was the only constructive, progressive thing she could do right then. It came much easier than she had expected—she was very strong and very stubborn, and it was a matter of pride, really—and then there were all those little children looking at her with their big, dark eyes, so lovingly. She was teaching class scrupulously, every morning, and now that her Spanish was perfect the children's English was getting better too. She loved them. She just loved children. They had a very good influence on her. It was like being herself again. She still drank too much, but one couldn't do everything at once. All her courage suddenly came back to her and her looks improved considerably. The American Vice Consul's wife was again inviting her—they had almost dropped her, she realized that now. And it was just as well that she managed to pull herself together, for José was beginning to need her as he had never needed her before.

His political star was now shining bright and it was clear that great things were ahead for him. The old regime was living its last days. José had thrown his support behind General Carriedo, who was quite unknown outside military circles, but who was a weak man, graft-ridden, and with a sordid past that made him vulnerable and submissive. Everybody was backing him because everybody expected to control him. Nancy was still shocked when she remembered how disgraceful the old regime had been. The capital was perhaps the most brazenly open vice center in the Western Hemisphere. The United Nations narcotics commission denounced it as the chief supplier of drugs. The blue circuit, once confined to the streets behind the Liberator's Square, had invaded the whole city. Pornographic pictures were openly shown in the theaters everywhere. The gamblers and the gangsters from all over the world had moved in, and new casinos were being built all the time. It was the smuggling center for gold, diamonds and embargo goods. Of course, things couldn't be changed overnight: it was a lifetime job, really, and even when José became truly influential, he had to proceed very slowly, so as not to ruin the nation's economy and the tourist trade—it was such a poor country with its natural resources hardly tapped, one just couldn't go about throwing everything out of balance. And then, in spite of all those rumors and of certain American papers who soon began to call him "a dictator," he didn't even hold any official position in the government; he was just respected and listened to, and he couldn't break with the past with one stroke of a magical wand.

Anyway, the old regime was overthrown, General Carriedo was elected President and José's best friends found themselves in office. There was great joy among the population, firecrackers, dancing, and she mixed with the people in the streets and danced with them; the Liberation had come, and a new life was opening for everyone. It was the best thing that had ever happened in this country. She was still teaching every morning, not so much because of what she was accomplishing for the children as because of what the children were accomplishing for her; she needed them. In their presence and in their loving eyes, she was finding herself, she was recapturing all her dreams and hopes and integrity. It was very complicated and difficult, for she was busy now with much greater things, but she never missed her class. And every morning, when she was driven there by her chauffeur, there was always a respectful crowd of parents waiting at the school's door just to see her. And often there were press cameramen and, once or twice, American reporters.

She began at once to have things done; it was entirely due to her influence that the government had at last decided to build a new telephone system in the country.

She had always been almost in despair about the country's telephones; whenever she tried to reach José on the line, it was like struggling through some jungle of inefficiency. The new government had been in power only a few weeks when she began to talk to José about it. She was meeting with certain difficulties when she tried to see him, which was only natural, as he was now an extremely busy man. But he did see her, and once more she was a little surprised by his strange manner with her; he looked almost worried, and even—yes, it was of course, ridiculous, but he did look almost scared.

At first, he wouldn't listen. He simply couldn't understand why this country *had* to have a modern telephone system. She pleaded and pleaded—it just had to be, ab-so-lute-ly. It was the first and most urgent thing to do. It would put the country on the map as a modern, civilized, progressive place. The telephone system, that was the first thing on which the Americans would judge the progress made by the new government, and its efficiency. The last argument seemed to impress him, and he suddenly said: "Okay, okay. I will see to it. You just take it easy."

It was almost as if he were willing to do anything to get rid of her, but of course, it only seemed that way; he really did it because he loved her. If she ever needed the proof, there it was. Of course, his enemies had immediately begun to grumble and tried to imply that the new telephone connections that the government was building now at top speed, with American money and American technicians, had no other purpose behind them than to facilitate the work of the police and to tighten the control over the distant provinces, so that the dictator's hand could reach everywhere. But some people are always like that, negative and cynical about everything. And she was already planning even greater things. She was going to see to it that the capital had a good public library, a symphony orchestra and a modern art museum. She considered the art museum particularly important, but she realized that it would take a lot of explaining, so she decided that it should come last. Actually, a modern art museum like the one she had seen in New York, even if much smaller and more modest—one had to begin somewhere—was absolutely essential. They could make attendance compulsory for schoolchildren, and then it would be wonderful to establish a direct contact between the peasants of the provinces and modern art. It could spark a real cultural renaissance.

In the beginning, there would probably be some resistance to the idea, and they would have to make it compulsory for peasants to visit the museum. They could be brought along in Army trucks. A day spent at the museum would be considered a day's work, and they would be paid. Something wonderful was bound to emerge from this confrontation between simple, noble, primitive souls and the great modern achievements of contemporary artists. It was the creative thing to do. She wrote a long letter to her grandmother about this, and also to some of her school friends, and she sent them a picture of herself that had appeared in the social section of the capital's biggest newspaper. She was beginning to see herself as a sort of Evita Perón, only, of course, very different, because everything was to be done through a strictly democratic process of persuasion and education.

She felt a little worried when the new government— some people were openly referring to José as the country's "strong man"—gave the American Ambassador forty-eight hours to leave the country, but then the United States behaved quite decently about it and increased their economic aid, and soon they had a new ambassador who was very nice to her and invited her to cocktails; they had probably heard about the telephone system there.

She knew now that she would never be First Lady of the land; only her cook and maids still believed that. And this stood to reason; José couldn't marry an American, not in his new position, it would be a political suicide; anti-Americanism was the catchword now. But he still treated her in his strange, respectful way, almost with shyness, behaving as if he were in church, or perhaps as if she had an evil eye—she just couldn't make head nor tail of it.

She was then trying to get him to build a public library in the capital, but he couldn't see the point at all. It was quite by accident that she had found a way of convincing him.

She had been pleading with him, explaining how important it was to make good literature accessible to all. It was the best way to prove that his regime was democratic, and that it was taking care of the population's most basic and urgent needs. He just shrugged.

"If you don't build the library," she had told him finally in despair, "I think I'll just die. You don't realize how vulnerable your position is now. The whole world has its eyes on you. They are beginning to call you a 'strong man' and this is always very bad. You know what I did yesterday? You'll probably think it childish, but I went with my maid to the Santa María Church and prayed to the Holy Virgin for you."

José suddenly looked scared.

"You leave me alone," he told her, in a low, tense voice. "You leave me alone, you understand? Ab-so-lute-ly. I don't need no prayers."

But he gave the order to build the public library at once,

and what was even more important to her was the discovery that she truly had a power over him. And, although
she didn't quite yet know what there was behind it, she
now knew how to get things done. She began to work on
the symphony orchestra at once. The people loved music,
it would make their lot better and it was important to silence
those who were accusing the government of being indifferent to the needs of the masses. With a large symphony
orchestra hall built right in the center of the city, in the
Square of the Liberator, everybody would see that the
people were getting something for their money. It would
stand there like a symbol of progress and a promise of other
marvelous things to come. There would be special charity
performances to raise funds for a musical academy and to
encourage young, struggling artists. There were some ugly
rumors around—all this nonsense about the students being
against the government—a musical academy would mean
that the cultural minority was properly looked after. She
knew that José had made a lot of enemies, simply because
he was fighting corruption and the old ways of the country;
there was some talk about members of the opposition being
thrown in jail and some of them were even said to have
vanished mysteriously. She felt deeply that a symphony
orchestra was exactly what was needed and that it would
somehow make everything look all right.

He refused.

It was then that she hit upon the idea. She did it instinctively; it was a hunch. She still hadn't realized how profoundly superstitious he was. It was merely some childish
wish to challenge him and to annoy him because he was
so stubborn; she remembered how he had become furious
when she told him that she was praying for him.

"If you don't give me the symphony orchestra," she

warned him solemnly and defiantly, "I'll be on my knees at the Cathedral tomorrow morning, praying to Our Lady for you, praying for your salvation."

He gaped at her wide-eyed and then suddenly struck her. It had never happened before and she was frightened. She just couldn't understand why he did it. Tears came to her eyes, but she still managed to smile.

"I'll be praying for you as long as I live," she told him.

He grabbed his hat and almost ran away.

The next morning her black Cadillac took her, her head properly covered with a mantilla, to the Cathedral, and there the whole population watched her as she kneeled before the altar praying. She was a Presbyterian, and anyway she was an agnostic, but it didn't matter. It was one of those small compromises one had to accept if one wanted to get things done. She couldn't understand what was on José's mind, why he was so frightened of her praying for him, but she was going to have her symphony orchestra, come rain, hell or high water. She sank to her knees before the altar and prayed.

In the afternoon, José broke into her house completely drunk, and beat her up.

"You just leave me alone, you silly cow," he shouted. "If you ever set foot in that church again I'll have a stone attached to your neck and throw you into the ocean. Stop praying for me, you bitch. You'll ruin me. Mind your own business."

She still couldn't understand what it was all about and why he was so scared. All she knew was that she could now have her own way with him, that she was going to get what she wanted. She looked at him with a triumphant smile.

"If you don't build a symphony orchestra hall," she shouted, "I'll have the Papal nuncio conduct a special service for you and he'll have them pray for you in Rome too."

The Cujon's face was green with terror and panic. He beat her up badly. In fact, for several days she couldn't appear in school to teach her class, and even then she had to hide her eye under dark glasses. But she got her symphony orchestra all right. The government, at that time, was trying to get another big loan from the United States, and they felt that the news of a symphony orchestra hall would be well received in Washington and would prove that the American funds were being used properly for the benefit of the people.

The news that the strong man had an American mistress began to appear in the magazines back home, discreetly at first, and she received two or three newspapermen who were very tactful and considerate, and who listened to her with great interest as she tried to explain the country to them, warning them not to judge it from the conventional American point of view. It had a wonderful democratic future ahead of it—and she took them herself, in her car, to look at the symphony orchestra hall, which was being built and would soon be ready.

And so, naturally, she was absolutely crushed and horrified when a big national magazine in New York published an article about her, with a series of pictures, under the title: "The American Girl Friend of a Dictator." Not that the article was insulting, but then it was so unfair to call José a dictator—he hadn't even been given an official position, which was shocking—and the pictures of her were simply awful. She couldn't possibly look like that. She was only twenty-five, and they must have deliberately used the light in such a way as to make her face appear tragic. Yes, that's how her face looked in the pictures—tragic. But it didn't matter. She was going ahead full speed all the same —except that she didn't quite know what to write to her grandmother. The symphony orchestra hall was soon ready and she had very good pictures taken of herself on opening night, as they presented some sort of medal to her for the part she had played in the cultural progress of the country. It was all very good for American prestige. She was now planning a new university and a new ministry of education—the present building was simply awful, and the budget was nonexistent.

A childhood sweetheart came to visit her with his bride, and she received them wearing the Blue Ribbon of the Order across her breast. She talked all night to them excitedly, basking in their admiration, begging them not to believe the ugly rumors spread by the exiles and not to judge everything in this country by American standards, to try to understand and to sympathize. But when they left her, she just sobbed and sobbed; she didn't know quite why, because everything was simply wonderful and she was truly having things done. Maybe she was just lonely and overwrought. She decided to start working on José at once, to get him to build a museum of modern art, and then set about organizing an Impressionist exhibition at the old university, to be followed by a Picasso showing; this was indispensable for José's prestige and would silence all the beastly rumors that were flying.

The students were restless and unco-operative. They did need a new university, the poor things. She knew that José was more and more impressed with her, though he tried not to show it, and even sometimes seemed to avoid her. But when she insisted, he always gave in. He always tried to appease her if there was a difficulty; it was enough for her to begin to cry, or to tell him that if he didn't build the university she would kill herself—but that didn't mean that she would abandon him, because she was going to pray for him in Heaven—and he would be furious at first, then scared, and sometimes even spit on the floor in some sort of superstitious fear, but in the end she always got what she wanted—he did love her deeply, even though he was completely unable to communicate his feelings, the poor boy, he was so repressed and ingrown. If she remained for some time without trying to see him or without telephoning him, he would always come to see her. He didn't want her to be unhappy and he was always asking, in a rather mocking but uncertain way, if she had been to church again; and when she felt sick, one day, he became truly scared, and had the best doctors attend to her. She was quite moved to see how worried he looked and tried to reassure him and told him half-jokingly and perhaps also to tease him a little: "After all the good I have tried to do, I am sure I'll go to Heaven," and it upset him so much that he flew into a rage and threatened to hang the doctors if they didn't save her. She always kept his favorite cigars ready, and in the end he would always visit her, always unannounced, and sometimes with friends, as if he were checking on something. Maybe he was just jealous. Sometimes he would even bring one of his numerous girl friends. She didn't mind. The girls always treated her with great respect and they were shy and embarrassed with her; it was quite touching. She did resent it a little, though, when she heard now and then that he had an American or a European mistress, but she almost always managed to make friends with them, asking them to tea and taking them to see the sights. Anyway, those affairs never lasted long because the girls were always so conventional and hollow, usually some poor performers from the night club or some Hollywood glamour nonsense. They had really nothing to offer him and in the end there was always a moment, which she rather enjoyed, when they would come up to her and cry and beg her to help them make up with José, who had left them, or to ask her to get them some money and arrange their passage home. And then she would get hold of José immediately and explain to him quite firmly that he really couldn't behave like that, in his important position; that he had to treat the girls decently, even when it was all over, not just throw them away like broken toys.

XIV

THE CAR was jumping over the stones and the valleys were already in shadows; the evangelist shuddered; it was getting chilly. The dummy Ole Jensen was staring at the girl over his master's shoulder.

"The man seems to be a living denial of every human decency," Dr. Horwat said gruffly.

She shook her head.

"He's only a dreamer, really. Do you know what the talent agencies all over the world call him? The star-eater. They mean only, of course, that they find it almost impossible to keep up with his impatient, pressing demands for new talent: he devours in one season everything they have to offer, and still keeps looking for something more exciting, something strange, unique, that has never been seen before. I have done what I could for him—I have appointed myself his guardian angel, so to speak—for me, love is the greatest and the only sure magic there is. But let's face it: I have failed. There is some very primitive longing in him —a deep, superstitious craving for the supernatural—he seeks it relentlessly and naïvely. It took me some time to discover and to accept as a fact that he actually thought that a man could sell his soul to the devil, you know. Isn't it incredible?"

"He seems to have succeeded very well," the evangelist said.

The girl looked at him reproachfully.

"Now, really, Dr. Horwat. You are an educated man, a

distinguished man. You cannot possibly believe in such nonsense."

"My dear child, everything you have just told me merely confirms my opinion that, as I have always thought and said, the devil is an actual presence, a constant and living menace to all of us," the young evangelist said, rather emphatically.

Over the ventriloquist's shoulder, the dummy watched him with his critical eye.

"Well, a fellow has got to believe in something," he remarked.

Dr. Horwat gave the object a crushing glance.

"And may I add," he continued, "that we are seeing the devil ourselves right now—we are looking at him with our own eyes."

The dummy uttered a brief, scornful laugh.

"No such thing," he said. "Nothing but phonies, bloody liars, all of them. Nobody has ever managed to sell his soul, my kind sir. Just another one of those false hopes we are being fed."

Without quite knowing how, young Dr. Horwat suddenly found himself in a violent argument with a ventriloquist's dummy—but then he had always been better at speaking than at listening, and it didn't matter much to him to whom he spoke, particularly when he felt deeply about the matter. They were all in bad need of some straightening out in their thinking—in dire need of spiritual help. He went on talking for a while with a deep conviction and felt better.

"You just cannot deny this fact," he insisted. "The evil presence is as real as you and I."

The dummy shook once more with disagreeable laughter.

"All bums," he said. "All fakes and crooks. You never

meet the real thing—just a lot of middlemen with big mouths, peddling nonexistent goods. They keep promising, but they cannot deliver. No real talent here below, my kind sir. Just a few poor tricksters, like your humble servant."

"Our greatest thinkers have known this elementary truth," Dr. Horwat concluded, raising his voice to silence the dummy. "Goethe himself—"

"A bum," the dummy said. "A crook, a liar. Feeding people false hope under the guise of poetry, like all of them. Anyway, he missed his point completely. The truth about Faust, my dear sir, is not at all that he had sold his soul to the devil. That is merely a reassuring lie. The truth about good old Faust and about all of us who are trying so hard, is that there is no devil to buy our soul. . . . All phonies. A lot of con men, impostors, cheap tricksters, fakes. They keep promising, but cannot deliver. No real talent. That's my tragedy, as an artist, my kind sir—and it is breaking my little heart."

The dummy sighed and let its head sink low over his master's shoulder. The girl laughed, leaned forward, and patted him on the head. Ole Jensen cheered up considerably.

"That was an awfully nice thing to do," he said.

Dr. Horwat permitted himself to shrug. "I disagree."

"All I can say then, Dr. Horwat," the girl remarked, "is that I am not at all surprised that José has given such a large sum for your spiritual crusade. He often listened to the recordings of your speeches and it always seemed to do him a lot of good. I don't know if you realize it or not, but you've helped him a great deal. You have confirmed all his superstitions and dispelled all doubts he might have felt. In his eyes, you're a great American, a thinker, a famous, educated man—and if even you could claim that the devil is a true living presence on earth, then he knew that he had been right all the time."

Dr. Horwat calmly crossed his arms on his chest.

"This is known as heresy," he said. "I have never told him to follow the evil one."

"Well, he seems to have figured that out for himself," the girl said with a sigh. "He wanted all the good things— the bad things, you would say—the earth had to offer, and he craved for magic. It is a craving that runs strong in the Indian blood—and in some so-called civilized people's blood too, it seems."

The evangelist let pass the implication.

José received a constant flow of cables from various talent agencies, reporting to him in enthusiastic, tempting terms some new and awe-inspiring display of superhuman powers.

There was a man who could turn somersaults with twelve full glasses balanced on a tray. There was a contortionist who could fit himself into a hat box. There was a Turk who could swallow flaming swords and dance on burning charcoals. . . . That was as far as it ever went—and, after staring gloomily at the latest cable, José would swear, grab a bottle and get drunk, out of some deep longing or despair.

She remembered particularly well the juggler Santini, perhaps because José had never tired of watching him.

Santini was a wiry, graying little man from a family of Sicilian jugglers that went as far back as the seventeenth century. His act was recognized as unique. He stood on one foot, on the tip of a champagne bottle, with the other leg bent behind him, keeping three rings in continuous rotation around its calf, with another bottle balanced on his forehead and two large rubber balls on top of it, while at the same time juggling with nine balls. There was a deep, almost religious hush in the audience when he performed, and even the usual drunks fell suddenly silent. But it was the expression on José's face that Nancy kept watching, more than the juggler's act. It was an expression of naïve wonder and of almost scared delight. The great man whom everybody feared was gone, and there was only an Indian there, craving for his long-lost gods and fulfilling his thirst for the supernatural. Talacoate, who could raise mountains and blow fire from the entrails of the earth, Ijmujin, who could give eternal life, Aratuxin, who chose kings among men . . . She wished she could take his dreaming head in her arms and press it against her heart.

Santini stood there in his incredible defiance of the laws of nature, of balance and gravity, and sometimes, in a su-preme gesture of mastery, he would step even further and balance a stick on his nose—a proud pioneer beyond the frontiers of the possible.

It was a moment of great human triumph. After the per-formance, José always invited the artist to join them. Off the floor, when his act was over, Santini was strangely with-drawn and silent. His eyebrows raised in the middle, above the dark, little eyes, conferred on his face an expression of perpetual sadness.

One day, José asked him a question.

"There is no secret," Santini answered. "Just hard work. No private life, no happiness, no love, just hard work. And you never succeed."

"You did," she told him.

"Oh, no," the little Sicilian said. "I have failed. You see, for years now I've been trying to do my act while juggling ten balls. But I've never achieved that, never. I honestly think I would sell my soul just to be able to do it once. My grandfather did, or so they say."

He got up and bowed.

"And so, *señor*, if you know someone who's looking for a soul and is willing to pay the right price—the tenth ball, it isn't asking too much—tell him to contact my agent. Tell him I am willing. All true artists are. Good night."

José never watched the juggler's act again.

Charlie Kuhn was constantly scouting the world for him for new talent.

There was only one artist whom José, in spite of all his efforts, had never been able to book. He was a mysterious Englishman who went by the name of "Jack" and who was said to perform a fantastic act of levitation. No one knew much about him. He had no agent and he seemed to shun notoriety, choosing obscure, cheap dives in the remote corners of the earth to make his rare appearances. Some agents claimed that he didn't exist at all—that he was, as Charlie Kuhn had ventured to suggest, nothing but a legend, a projection—an image of the impossible, created by all the frustrated, cynical and yet secretly yearning talent scouts in the world. But for José this was nothing but a smart excuse for the agent's failure to get the artist for him, and this fellow "Jack" was assuming in his mind almost mythical proportions. He talked about him constantly. And often, as he sat in his night club, half-crazed by alcohol and by his longing, watching with a mocking scorn, almost with hatred, some wretched performer twist, jump, turn somersaults or stand on his head, he would squeeze his glass until it burst in his hand and she knew that this fellow "Jack" was on his mind again.

And yet there were so many things happening that required his complete attention.

One morning Nancy was awakened by a roar outside her

house. The maid rushed in, screaming. She had hardly the time to put on her dressing gown when a stone broke through the window, and then another. A crowd of peasants from the near-by market had gathered in front of the gates; they were shouting insults and threats, and now they were beginning to throw stones. At first she didn't think there was anything personal in it—it was just one of those anti-American outbursts. She was the most prominent American resident in the capital, much better known than the Ambassador, because of all the things that she had done for the country, so it was only natural that they should have thought of her first. In a way, it was even flattering. They didn't riot in front of the American Embassy: they rioted in front of her house. It just went to prove that she was truly considered as representing America in this country. She had even smiled, with a certain amount of satisfaction; it would make the American Ambassador livid. And then the police came, and the crowd was soon dispersed. She didn't give it much thought, until the trials began. It was really terrible. It came as a complete and most bewildering shock to her. She couldn't understand. The poor Minister of Education had been thrown in jail and then tried, just because he had allowed the building of the new university, of the public library, of the symphony orchestra hall. Apparently, it was now considered as a waste of people's money, a misuse of government funds. She sobbed and sobbed, and wished she were dead. It showed such terrible ingratitude. She tried everything she could to save the man, but they sentenced him to death for sabotage and waste, and they shot him. She pleaded to be allowed to appear in court, to testify on the man's behalf, to explain that this should be considered her fault—that it was she who had been actually instrumental in the creation of those progressive and cultural developments. But she couldn't do it. José wouldn't allow her, and he was right. It would have ruined him. He couldn't possibly admit that his American mistress had such an influence over him. So there was nothing she could do about it, except cry. And one couldn't even blame those poor people, actually. They were so completely uneducated, so far behind, they were so deeply embedded in their ignorance, that they simply couldn't see what tremendous benefits for their country and for their country's prestige abroad and for the future of their children it all meant. They didn't even seem to understand that they were being saved from Communism. One just had to work harder, explaining, informing, educating. What this country needed right now was a Public Information Service, run by intelligent, cultured people who would condition the masses psychologically for the next step on the road of progress.

José had been awfully nice about it, really. Although she had almost, unwittingly, damaged his career, he took her on a triumphant political tour of the country. They went everywhere. It was most exciting; she had a wonderful time. He had never before taken her officially anywhere with him. At night, there were often volleys of shots; people were enjoying themselves. She did feel a certain uneasiness about this shooting, but José always reassured her, and then all those events had upset her a great deal and she was getting very nervous and always imagining terrible things.

And wherever they went, even in the most distant provinces, there was always the telephone. When she was tired, or anxious, or when the shooting at night made her imagine all sorts of ridiculous things, she would look at the telephone and touch it, almost caress it, and feel reassured and know that it had not been all for nothing, after all.

XV

THE ROAD twisted along among black lava rocks, and at each turn, there was a screech of tires, a cloud of dust, and Charlie Kuhn was once more finding himself staring at the precipice below. He had given up trying to understand what was happening. García had offered them no explanation. He had just shouted that there was political trouble in the capital, and then he had screamed angrily at them and pushed him into the car with the others. In the confusion and panic of the moment, with motorcyclists dashing around them and García hollering and menacingly brandishing his gun, and also, perhaps, because they had huddled instinctively together like scared sheep, they had squeezed themselves into two Cadillacs, in considerable physical discomfort, but feeling a little better for company.

The Indian woman sat in the back of the car, next to Mr. Sheldon, the lawyer; a squat, almost square figure, chewing her leaves with a contented grin. Charlie Kuhn had heard a lot about the hallucinatory effect of the mastala plant; it was said to be similar to that of the teonacatl mushrooms of Mexico, the "mushrooms of God." They induced hilarity and procured heavenly visions; the Zatopec Indians used them for their religious ceremonies: they were the true and the cheapest opium of the people. From time to time, Mrs. Almayo shook with merry, happy laughter and, considering that she had been ordered shot by her own son, her laughter had something evil and almost diabolical about it. At each of these outbursts, the lawyer, Mr. Sheldon, gave her a pained look.

Little Mr. Manulesco, the green, white and red sequins of his costume glittering in the sun, the white flour of his face shining with sweat, and the little peaked clown's hat still on his head, sat next to the driver. He looked back toward Charlie Kuhn, his soft brown eyes full of anguish and gentle reproach, trying to avoid the ghastly view of the abyss that at each turn was claiming them like some gaping, hungry monster. There was no more depressing sight, Charlie thought, than a musical clown in broad daylight.

"I can't understand why he would do such a thing to us," Monsieur Antoine was saying. "The man has always shown such respect for talent."

"There's a rebellion in the capital," Charlie Kuhn said.

"What can that have to do with us? Do you think they're taking us to some secluded spot in the mountains and there—?" Mr. Manulesco's face seemed suddenly even whiter.

"I don't know."

He had never expected to find Almayo in trouble so quickly—even though the papers in the States had been for some time referring to armed guerrilla bands in the mountains. He had flown to visit him only two months earlier to discuss new acts for his club, and everything seemed under control then. The latest starlet from Hollywood was sitting on a couch in a corner, humming a Frank Sinatra tune—José had always liked to have the freshest crop in Hollywood flown to him. Usually, the girls wanted only yachts, diamonds and mink coats, but this one was different; she had asked for a collection of Impressionist paintings. When the talent agency had reported her terms to him, Almayo as usual had said, "Okay, okay," and he obviously did not have the slightest idea what Impressionist paintings were. They turned out to be damned expensive, and he had bawled out Charlie Kuhn as soon as he saw him. The girl had been told that Almayo was only a play-boy but, judging by her worried appearance, she was prob-ably no longer quite certain that she had done the right thing in coming. She was humming the Sinatra tune to reassure herself, and as a gesture of defiance, even though that fellow didn't probably know who Frankie was, as she told Charlie Kuhn later. Uneducated bastard.

"Nice to see you, Charlie," Almayo said. "What's the latest dirt about me in the United States?"

"There was something in the papers about the man Raphael Gómez," Charlie Kuhn answered. "They say he is leading a guerrilla outfit in the southern mountains."

Almayo nodded. "Sure, he is. He's well armed and he has good people with him, and I'm scared. I'm quite scared, Charlie. I'm losing my grip, see?"

He threw his head back and roared with laughter, and Charlie found himself grinning foolishly, although he did not quite know why.

"Good, clean-living boy, Raphael Gómez," Almayo said. "A hero. So they like him, eh?"

"Well, you know how they are back there in the States, José. They always pitch for the underdog."

"The underdog, eh? Raphael Gómez, the underdog . . ." He shook his head. "There's only one thing about it, Charlie. About that underdog. You know who sent Raphael Gómez into the Sierra? You know who gave him the weapons, supplies and a few good men? I did."

Charlie Kuhn remained speechless, while the macaws once more started their piercing laughter behind him, and he felt the monkey tearing at his pants.

"Raphael Gómez is one of my men. I set him up in the mountains. I spread the news that he was out to get me, to overthrow the tyrant and establish a good, clean-living democracy. And you know why? You know why I did it?"

"No," Charlie Kuhn said. "I'm in the entertainment field, not in politics."

"Because every lousy dog who is against me in this country will try to join him. He acts like a magnet for every son-of-a-bitch who hates my guts and is out to get me. They send him messages—and the messages come back to me, so I get the names. Well, you can imagine what's going to happen to them when the crop is ready. I have my troops sitting around just waiting for Gómez to give me the sign. I have learned one or two tricks in my life, Charlie. I have what it takes. I, too, have talent. Any new girls back there for me in Hollywood?"

"There's one who's getting quite famous, but she's under age, so she comes out only with her mother."

"Well, okay, who cares? Let her bring her mother. I wish I could go to the States myself, but I somehow feel they don't like me there. But they like Raphael Gómez."

He threw his head back and roared again, and then looked at Charlie Kuhn seriously once more.

"Now, let's get down to business. Have you got him for me?"

Charlie Kuhn often wished that he had never told Almayo about that fellow "Jack." He had heard about him for the first time from the Tivoli Gardens in Copenhagen, several years ago. The Gardens manager had told him that he had never seen anything like this in his whole life. He was an illusionist of an extraordinary skill, probably a mass hypnotist, for there could be no other explanation for the extraordinary mastery of his act.

The manager had never heard of him before, and yet the fellow must have been around for a long, long time; he looked quite old, he couldn't be a beginner. He had a noble mane of white hair, a short, white Spanish beard, and spoke excellent, refined English. And he had a little Cockney chap with him as an assistant.

His act was unique. He would step out onto the stage, dressed in tails with a top hat and a cane, and sit down on a chair. He would sit there a moment, quite a while, until the public would begin to stir impatiently and then he would lift his cane and make a large, commanding gesture. And then—well, it was just extraordinary. The chair would rise into the air, quite fast, sometimes as high as fifty feet. The height varied each night. And there he would remain seated, floating in mid-air without any visible or invisible support. The manager of the Tivoli was absolutely positive about it.

But there was more to it. That fellow "Jack" would hang there for a while and then, suddenly, he would vanish— yes, vanish into thin air, literally—and the chair would remain empty for a while—a crazy, bewildering, impossible thing, that had the public goggle-eyed—and then "Jack" would reappear, sitting in the same position as before, his legs crossed, with a glass of wine in his hand or smoking a cigar. And, slowly, the chair would sink to the floor, and that was all.

The act lasted only a few minutes and it left the audience completely stunned, unable to move or applaud and sitting there in complete silence. Of course, there had been other levitation acts before: clever tricks, talented variations on the old Indian rope act, but to the best of the manager's knowledge—and he had been in this business for fifty years—there had never been anything like this. Mass hypnotism, of course; he had secretly tried to have pictures taken of the performance, but it didn't work out: the photographer always somehow forgot to press the button, and when he had himself tried to film it with a hidden movie camera, all he got was a black goat standing in the middle of the floor.

Charlie Kuhn knew the Dane's impish sense of humor, and he didn't mind a joke himself, so he smiled politely. He also knew the great secret dream that always lived in every member of the profession; they would all lie and tell you the tallest tales, under the pretext of joking, wishing they were true. They were all addicts of make-believe, and when they lied, it was for illusion's sake, to bolster their own faith, and out of sheer longing. But he had checked the story carefully and the act appeared to be truly exceptional. There was only one hitch: he had never been able to contact that fellow "Jack."

He did not seem to have an agent, only his assistant, a shabby, dirty and sarcastic man who looked after him and took care of the props. Actually, the manager explained, it was because of his assistant that "Jack" had had to leave town in a hurry. He was an exhibitionist, and was caught by the Danish police in some very unsavory circumstances. They were forced to leave town, which was a pity. It was a great act. The greatest.

Charlie Kuhn knew that a performer of such talent couldn't just get lost and that he would appear soon enough in some circus, music hall or night club. There were not that many good acts around.

But it was six months before he heard of "Jack" again. It was obvious that, for some reason or other, the man was determined to remain anonymous, and that he was only performing his trick when he needed the money badly.

His next appearance was, of all places, in Mérida, Mexico, in some cheap, strip-tease joint. It simply did not make sense why he chose to appear there when he could command any price in the best night clubs in Paris or Las Vegas. It was exactly the same performance as the one that had been described to Charlie Kuhn in Copenhagen, except that he did not rise quite so high in the air as the Tivoli manager would have it, not more than fifteen feet, which was incredible enough.

By that time, the whole entertainment circuit throughout the world was already buzzing with the news, and they all tried to book the fellow. Charlie Kuhn rushed to Mérida. He found several talent scouts from Paris, Hamburg and Las Vegas. He himself had in his pocket a furious cable from Almayo and he did not feel like getting on the dictator's wrong side; he felt both excited and worried.

To make the matters even worse, the man who ran the joint, and who had never been the object of such attention before, said that "Jack" had left town already, and that no one knew where he had gone. If the fellow was trying to build himself up as a big mystery, he was certainly succeeding. But he did not need to do that, as they were all ready to get him at any cost.

They tried to pump the bistro owner for more information about the act and about the fellow, but the Mexican didn't know much and cared even less. A very fine, noble-looking *caballero*, speaking excellent Spanish—that was as far as his description went. He always appeared very depressed when he had finished his act, and when the café owner complimented him, he shook his head sadly and sighed.

"I hate these cheap tricks," he said, and his assistant, a strange little fellow, laughed.

"Well, you have to earn your living like everybody else, now, Jack," he told him.

The artist gave him a crushing look, but said nothing. It was a strange thing to see these two together, and the café owner wondered a little how they came to be partners: such a noble-looking, distinguished *señor,* always so immaculate in his dress, and that very unpleasant one, with a cruel, mean face, and yellowish eyes, who always seemed to make fun of his partner. He had a very peculiar habit, that fellow had: he would take a box of matches out of his pocket, light a match, watch it burn out and then he would hold the match close to his nose and inhale deeply and with great delight the slightly sulfurous smell of the burning chemical—it was a most unpleasant habit, although the café owner could not quite say why; it was just strange and unusual.

How did the local public react to the performance? Well, they did not care for it too much. They usually came for the girls—the joint specialized in strip tease and that was what they wanted, and they were impatient with anything that delayed the girls from coming on stage. Sure enough, when that man "Jack" sat in a chair and the chair slowly rose fifteen feet into the air—yes, something like fifteen feet—when he suddenly vanished and the chair floated alone, and then he reappeared, drinking champagne from a glass, they applauded. They were also impressed with his tails—many of them had never seen such fine clothes before, and they liked it. But it was the girls that they really wanted.

Partout, the talent scout from Paris, looked at Charlie Kuhn, and the Las Vegas man, Fiddlestein, wiped the perspiration from his brow. It was incredible that such a performer should limit himself to dirty little joints in Godforsaken places, and the only explanation they had was that the man was truly in trouble with the police, and wanted to avoid attracting too much notice, while at the same time trying to make the best of it, and offering his act in unexpected places, never staying very long, always on the move.

Charlie Kuhn then flew to see Almayo, reporting his failure and trying to explain that he had done his best, and that it was not his fault. Almayo listened in awed silence. The agent had expected an outburst of fury, of rage, but when he finished speaking, José only stared at him for a moment with that animal gray-green light in his eyes.

"I want that fellow here, Charlie," he said at last, in a low voice. "I want him badly, you understand?"

"I'm doing what I can," Charlie said, uneasily. "No one has succeeded yet. The Lido in Paris didn't manage to book him. Las Vegas didn't. The South American circuit didn't get him. He has no agent, no contact. He just appears and disappears—like in his act. He comes to a place, offers an audition, they grab him—and then he's gone. He seems to be an amateur, not a pro at all. Or, more likely, he has some big problem with the police. Maybe he's on the run. But we'll get him."

"He'll be protected from the police here," Almayo said. "You let him know that. I'll pay him whatever he wants and he'll have complete security. Tell him that I guarantee that—I, Almayo. Do you think he has heard about me?"

"I'm sure he has," Charlie Kuhn said, soothingly. "The whole world knows your name, José. You are a great man now."

"Well, you'd better get him for me, Charlie."

But it was another four months till they caught up with "Jack" again—in the Bristol Palladium, on the west coast of England. Charlie Kuhn was so afraid of missing him again that he thought it preferable not to warn Almayo in case of failure. He had every reason to congratulate himself on his prudence for, when he arrived in Bristol and rushed to the Palladium—it was no more than twenty-four hours after receiving the cable—the man was gone.

This time, the manager was able to confirm Charlie's suspicions: the police were looking for the pair. They seemed to want them for practically everything in the world, he said. "I don't know what they have done—it must be something pretty big—but his assistant told me that they just had to go away."

Charlie stood there dejectedly, thinking of Almayo.

"How is his act?" he asked, finally.

"Terrific," the manager said. "Mass illusion, of course, but the best I ever saw. He came in to see me—with his assistant, a swarthy little fellow, quite unpleasant, who seems to be completely in charge—and they offered an audition. They performed for me right there on the stage, and I sat alone in the stalls. When I saw him rise vertically on his chair, I got goose flesh. There's nothing like it in the business, I can tell you: big talent—the greatest! What really got me was that vanishing trick. At one moment, he was there in mid-air, sitting comfortably, his legs crossed, and then suddenly he wasn't there, just the chair floating in space, and then—bang!—back again in the chair, back from nowhere, sipping brandy. And then slowly, very slowly, the chair sank to the ground and it was over.

"Of course, I knew it was easier to perform this kind of hypnotic trick on one man than on the whole audience, and I wondered a little how it would go—but he did it all right. We had a packed house and every one of them saw it just as I have described it to you. The best piece of business I ever saw. I went to talk to him in his dressing room after the act. A very strange chap. English, and a little pompous, speaking as if he had been reciting Shakespeare all his life. And very sad. After the performance, he would sit in his dressing room, his beard sunk to his chest, in a state of complete dejection. Of course, I suppose, he knew even then that they were looking for him—he had every reason to be dejected. When I congratulated him and told him what I thought of his act—that it was the greatest thing in show business—he gave me a peculiar, reproachful look and sighed deeply, and the next thing I knew there were tears in his eyes.

" 'I hate it,' he said.

"But then, you know how true artists are: never satisfied with themselves. And that nasty little Cockney bastard laughed, as if it all were a very good joke. A repulsive individual, dirty, unkempt and completely hostile, and he had a most filthy habit: he had a huge box of matches in his hand and he was lighting one match after the other and blowing it out, and inhaling the sulfur smell with delight.

"I kept on repeating that this was a great act. I didn't know what else to say. The old gent looked at me again and shook his head. 'Ah, my dear man,' he said. 'It's nothing, believe me. You should have known me before. You should have seen me earlier. There was nothing I couldn't do.' 'Yeah,' the little fellow snickered. 'Jack is a has-been. He's through. He's had it. There was a time when he was truly great—there was no one like him—the greatest. I can still remember it—he could make the earth shake, the sun stand still—just anything. Yes, those were the days.'

"I laughed," the manager concluded, "but I felt that he should have saved this sort of selling talk for the public at the door of the circus tents and country fairs. I felt sorry for that fellow 'Jack' when I learned that he was in trouble.

I suppose it was his assistant; he was so obviously a jailbird on the run. And now they are gone. Oh, well, the good thing about our profession is that we all live in hope that something even greater will turn up—that's what keeps us going, really."

Charlie Kuhn had at first decided to keep the news of "Jack's" latest appearance to himself, but then he thought better of it. He was too scared of Almayo to try to handle him. He flew back to the States and talked to him over the telephone and then, at the dictator's insistence, he took a plane and reported to him once more. He was amazed at the tortured, haunted expression on Almayo's face as he told him in details his latest failure and his conversation with the manager of the Bristol Palladium.

He wanted to tell him that he should be reasonable, that "Jack" was only a cheat like all the other magicians, conjurors, hypnotists whose endless procession he had watched on his night club floor, but he didn't dare. He suddenly felt that if he made such a remark, if he said: "Come on, José, you know that this fellow is only more clever than the others, with better hidden ropes, that he's a cheat, a trickster, like them all," José would get up and wring his neck. He needed to believe. He was willing to be cheated. In many ways, he was still a superstitious peasant—and they were the best audience in the world. And so he heard himself saying: "You know, his assistant claims that this fellow 'Jack' can make the sun stand still and the earth shake. Looks as if, this time, we've got something really big."

He laughed. But he was amazed by the expression on Almayo's face; the Indian looked stricken.

"Did he really say that?"

"What?"

"That he could make the sun stand still and the earth shake?"

Charlie Kuhn stirred uneasily, and was going to say: "Come on, José, it's only the usual talk of all the circus barkers in the world," but then he heard himself answer very seriously, as if talking to a child: "Yes, he did."

"I want him here," Almayo said, almost in a murmur. "Both of them. You find them for me, Charlie."

And now, as the car swished and jumped along the road, Charlie Kuhn fumbled in his pocket and stared at the cable he had received only twelve hours ago. He had got them for him all right, but it was probably much too late for José Almayo.

XVI

HE WENT to the window once more, looking for the planes: they should have started bombing the city a half-hour ago. But the sky was empty, and he had not heard one single explosion. It was all still there: the towering building of the new university, the symphony orchestra hall, the new wing of the ministry of education and, right in the middle of the city, the massive structure of the museum of modern art, next to the public library.

The American cow, he thought once more with superstitious anger. He could see her face so clearly that it almost scared him. She was the only living thing in the world that ever scared him. She had true goodness in her—but it had taken him some time to discover this because she was so willing in bed, and he did not think that the two could go together—and her goodness always touched in him his most superstitious chord.

He had tried to see her as little as possible, when he began to sense what there was in her. But when she was out of sight, he felt worried and frightened; he knew she was praying for him. He had tried to tell himself that after everything he had done it was unlikely that prayer could do him much damage. Still, one could never tell, and he had thought it more prudent to see her from time to time, so as not to make her desperate. It was like having a constant menace over his head.

He should have killed her long ago but that was the worst thing to do, the most dangerous and damaging. It was much safer to have her on earth than in Heaven, because that was where that stupid cow was going to go. That was where she was now, he was quite sure. He had done it in the end and now he felt scared. He could almost see her rushing about, pleading with them, begging them to forgive him.

If the priest were right and if God was truly merciful, she would save him; if anyone could, it would be she; then he would have wasted his life and all his efforts would have been for nothing. But he remembered suddenly that he had ordered his own mother shot and he slapped his thighs, roaring with laughter. This was something that even the American girl would not be able to explain and justify. No one had ever gone so far, he thought proudly. He would still make it.

The first sign that things were getting out of control came from Raphael Gómez and he had to admit that, for the first time in his life, he had been outsmarted. The young dog, whom he had so carefully hand-picked for his job as *agent provocateur*, whom he had himself set up with arms in the mountains to attract his enemies and then destroy them, had turned against him, and started a true guerrilla action in the south. He should never have chosen an educated man for the job. They were all full of tricks and treachery. What had happened was that the fellow had become intoxicated with all those articles written in the American press about his heroic stand. It had gone to his head.

But he had made some big mistakes himself, although the American girl had been responsible for most of them. The new roads and the modern telephone system reaching deep into the provinces made the people everywhere angry with the increased control exercised over them by the capital. They were accustomed to being left alone, remote, ignored, neglected and forgotten. The roads and the telephone restricted what they called their freedom and made them feel his iron hand on their necks. The telephone and the roads meant more police, more orders; it was more difficult to hide from the tax collectors, to refuse to be dragged into the Army, to keep their crops to themselves.

And then they had heard rumors of the waste in the capital, of strange buildings being erected there, government buildings—which meant more authority—the university, when they had no schools, and some even stranger and more wasteful things. They did not mind how much money he put in his own pocket. In a way, they even liked to know that one of them, a simple Cujon, had made good, and was living in such obvious luxury in a big palace overlooking the capital. They liked to watch him drive in splendid cars with his bejeweled mistresses. They identified themselves with him, and when they stood in the streets and watched his car go by, they nodded in approval and thought that perhaps their son would be sitting in his place one day.

But what had made their blood boil with anger and scorn was that he was wasting the money to build a new ministry of education, a symphony orchestra hall in place of the old bandstand where they used to listen every evening to music, a museum of modern art, and all those other unnecessary things which were an insult to their children and to their poverty. It was the new ministry of education and the new university that had really wounded them, for it was obvious that it was done only for the rich, for the children of the rich, not for the people.

And, of course, they knew that all this waste was the

American woman's idea, that she had a bad influence on their Cujon.

One morning, Almayo was informed that there were riots in the street just in front of the American girl's house. It was market day, and a crowd of peasants had gathered before the gate. They were shouting insults and they were beginning to throw stones.

Almayo recognized at once that he had made a big mistake, and he acted quickly. He had the Minister of Education arrested and tried for waste of government funds. Did he use American aid to build a symphony orchestra hall? Yes, he did. Did he use the government funds to build the public library and the museum of modern art? Yes, he did. And so on it went. The man could not have denied it, it was true. He was condemned for deliberate waste of government money and for sabatoging efforts to raise the standard of living of the masses, and he was shot.

Things had quieted down after that, but he knew his people well, and he knew that this was a test of strength, a showdown between him and them. If he had dismissed his American mistress then, or had tried her, or had her deported, they would have known that he was frightened of them and that they were gaining the upper hand. So he took her with him on his political tour of the country, as deep into the jungles and as high into the mountains as the roads could go. He made her wear her best clothes and her most beautiful jewels and, thus dressed, she went through the jungle and into the mud huts of the most distant and forsaken villages, as though she were going to a symphony orchestra performance.

In every village, the local chiefs brought fruit and presents for her, put garlands of flowers around her neck, and

Almayo stood by her side, puffing his cigar amiably.

But at night, as they rested in the huts equipped with Frigidaires which had been built especially for them, there was almost always the sound of shooting, and when she asked him once in a shaking voice what it was, he had replied: "People amusing themselves."

There had been a year of complete peace, but now his own Cujons were helping Raphael Gómez, and the Army had rebelled.

It was six o'clock, and there was still no sign of the Air Force and no sound of bombing, only sporadic shooting. If the Air Force joined with the rebels, there was nothing he could do. He would not even be able to get a plane to seek safety with the loyal forces under General Ramón in the southern peninsula.

He got up from the bed and went back to join the others. They were all here, all his good friends, whom the American press took so seriously, and to whom they referred as the "shadow cabinet."

There was Díaz, who had started in life as a student for the priesthood, but had been kicked out of the seminary and then had tried to become a psychoanalyst in Guatemala, and, after some mysterious trouble with the law, had ended up practicing hypnotism in music halls and as a circus magician, particularly expert at card tricks and the usual appearances of doves, parrots and rabbits from the bottom of a top hat. He still managed sometimes to amuse Almayo with his routines, and he kept him for luck more than for any other reason.

Then there was the Baron. They had discovered him sitting one night at the bar in the night club, and the next morning, when they opened the place, he was still sitting there, either completely drunk or just indifferent, no one really knew. In his pocket were seven passports of different nationality, all forged, some letters of introduction to Roman Cardinals, and his own picture cut out of a newspaper, but without any text, which didn't help much; he could be almost anything, an international criminal on the run or some great benefactor of humanity. He had not registered at any of the capital's hotels—he seemed to have turned in at the night club out of nowhere. Almayo liked the fellow. There was something strange about him. You could never tell.

The Baron—it was Radetzky who gave him his name—was a plump, red-faced man with a small gray mustache, blue eyes and bulging cheeks. He always appeared to be withholding either some indignant curse or some phenomenal burst of laughter. He wore a checkered suit, a yellow waistcoat, and a gray derby hat, and his shoes were protected by something that was called spats—Almayo had never seen that before. He was the cleanest-looking fellow he had ever seen, and he moved through life, through everything that befell him, through all the little practical jokes that they played on him, with a sort of mechanical dignity. Almayo could watch him for hours.

"Who do you think he is?" he would sometimes ask Radetzky in wonder, over the gambling table.

"An idealist, obviously," Radetzky said. "His eyes are raised so high that he can't be bothered to notice what happens to him. *Sprechen sie Deutsch, Herr Baron?*"

"What the hell is an idealist?" Almayo asked.

"An idealist," Radetzky explained, "is a son-of-a-bitch who thinks that the earth is not a good enough place for him."

Almayo had adopted the Baron and cared for him almost as much as for his pet monkey, just because he was strange.

He needed strangeness around him. It reassured him. There was an air of mystery about the fellow and that was good enough. He liked Díaz too—although he knew that he was a cheat, and that he would not hesitate to betray him. There was something truly rotten in him that seemed to hold some promise. Everything he had learned in life told him that honesty was a bad risk, that it was always on the losing side, that it didn't go with power, and so he had an almost physical distrust and fear of honesty.

And then there was Otto Radetzky, the man whom Hitler himself had trusted, a fellow who looked more dangerous than anyone he had ever known, with his flat face with two white scars across one cheek, and the pale blue eyes. He was an educated man, and he could talk about strange things, like idealism or paranoia—which was the scientific term for human greatness. Almayo liked having him around. He had met him in his night club one evening and they had some mutual friends in the Caribbean; he had told him impressive tales about that great man Hitler, whom he had known intimately, and he had soon become, for Almayo, an indispensable companion. He listened to the tales of fantastic armies conquering proud lands, of one man irresistibly imposing his will on millions of other men, worshiped and devotedly served and loved. Radetzky had some old newsreels flown in for him especially from Europe and America, and Almayo watched them with a fascination and a respect that he didn't even bother to conceal. He had been deeply impressed. Fantastic crowds in strange uniforms under a forest of banners, with burning torches in their hands, acclaiming one man who stood alone on the platform, so secure in his knowledge that he had the necessary backing, the necessary strength behind him.

"He had truly sold his soul to the devil," Radetzky told him one night.

But he didn't have to tell him. Almayo knew. This was obviously a man who had been blessed with talent, who had managed to strike a bargain. Images of lands conquered, of proud cities reduced to ashes, of great statesmen bowing their heads in submission, signing, approving, accepting; of young children presenting flowers to the master; of women's faces flushed with adoration—he had just had it in him, he had received the proper backing. This was about as high as any man could go. Without any doubt, this was real talent, and the man must have done a lot to deserve it. And yet, he had failed in the end, Radetzky explained. He had failed, just as Santini had never managed to catch the last ball. And he showed him the ruins of Berlin, and the bunker, and the charred bodies, and the utterly miserable, lonely folly of it all. But maybe, Almayo thought, it was simply because that man Hitler had not been bad enough.

He was looking at them with pleasure. The "shadow cabinet" was all here, and they didn't look too good now, any of them.

They were listening to the radio turned on full blast, and he knew at once that the station was still under government control. There was no mention of the fighting, no word about the rebellion, no sign of trouble. There were only local news and announcements, and although the speaker's voice was a little strained and at times shook slightly, the fellow was doing all right and he was making it sound good, Almayo thought. But then the announcer suddenly stopped in the middle of a sentence, there was a silence and a young, eager voice, trembling with emotion, came clearly through the loudspeaker:

"Death to the tyrant! Death to José Almayo! The corrupt and bloodthirsty government has been overthrown by the forces of the revolution. Long live the Liberator, Raphael Gómez!"

The monkey was jumping all over the place and throwing the papers around. Díaz had collapsed in a chair, pressing a handkerchief against his face. Radetzky looked at Almayo and grinned, and Almayo grinned back. The Baron sat perfectly still with an appearance of total unconcern—although Almayo suspected that he was merely immensely drunk, he felt a sort of grateful affection for the fellow; he was truly unlike anyone he had ever known. He took a good look at his "shadow cabinet."

"Well, this is it," Almayo said.

He went to his desk and emptied his box of cigars, filling his pockets with them.

"What about the Air Force?" Radetzky asked.

Almayo shrugged. It was then that they heard the drone of approaching planes. It was so sudden that they barely had time to realize what was happening. The explosions came in quick succession, one after another, and they found themselves lying on the floor, covered with glass flying from the windows, while the monkey jumped over them in panic and the macaws screamed piercingly. Only the Baron remained impassive in his chair, his eyebrows slightly raised with an expression of mild disgust.

"Let's go," Almayo said. "What the hell is that thing called anyway, the sacred right of asy—?"

"Yes," Radetzky said, "the sacred right of asylum."

"That's the word," Almayo said, getting up from the floor. "That's the tradition. That's what the South American embassies are for. We can still make it—perhaps."

He looked around for some things he could take with

him, and then remembered the Indian girl. He ran back to
his apartment to fetch her. They might have to stay many
weeks in the Embassy before getting a safe conduct, and
he did not want to get lonely. She was now dressed in the
American clothes he had given her. She stared at the broken
window but she did not seem upset. As he gestured to her,
she just looked at him and followed him. They rushed out
through the servants' entrance, taking only two bodyguards
with them, and jumped into the station wagon.

They had hardly started on their way when they saw
the low-flying aircraft approaching the Residence again.
Two police cars with sirens screaming sped past them,
stopped, turned in the narrow street, and then started to
chase them. There were people in the streets everywhere,
but the station wagon was going too fast. If there were some
shots, they didn't know it. They managed to reach the
Embassy and the door closed behind them, just as the police
were jumping out of their cars and stopping in front of the
gates, watching them helplessly, with Tommy guns in their
hands.

XVII

THEY STOOD in the middle of the entrance hall while Radetzky watched the movements of the troops outside through a peephole in the door. He could see a machine gun being put in position across the street facing the open gate, while more trucks of soldiers arrived and the police cars' sirens sounded deafeningly.

"Well, it's good to know that there is such a thing as international law," he said. "They can't come in here."

He turned away from the peephole and found himself looking at a group of people in evening clothes crowded at the door of the reception room to their right. Apparently, the Ambassador was entertaining guests for dinner. They stood completely still and stared at Almayo and at his bodyguards with the Tommy guns clutched in their hands. They were a distinguished crowd, and Almayo knew them all. Their wives had often tried anxiously, and a little desperately, to make polite conversation with him as they sat at his table. He had been often bored almost to insanity by them, trying to hold his temper.

There was the American Ambassador and his wife, who had so often tried to please him by talking ecstatically in her loud, hard voice about the wonderful things he had done for the country: the new university, the telephone, the symphony orchestra hall.

The Ambassador himself appeared to be completely shaken; his advisers had never warned him, and he had just written a report back home saying that the young fanatic, Raphael Gómez, could be completely discounted.

And then there was the British Ambassador, a tall, bald fellow with a clipped mustache, and his strange wife, who had once, sitting next to Almayo at a president's dinner, and after a total silence during the whole meal, turned to him and told him something should be done to protect the dogs and cats in the country, who were starving and neglected, and were roaming the streets and gardens in frantic, fearful and scared packs.

The French Ambassador was standing next to his wife, a glass in his hand—and as Almayo met his eye, he moved in front of her as if to protect her; he felt sure that it was just the sort of gesture that would be remembered by everybody afterward.

The rest of the guests—the Chief of Protocol at the Ministry of Foreign Affairs, and the First Secretary from one of the Latin embassies, who was there with his mother, one of those black-haired, dark-eyed, ripe Spanish ladies that seemed to be an indispensable ornament of every official party Radetzky had ever attended—still held their glasses in hand, making only those motions that could either pass unnoticed or would seem completely natural. None of them were trying to do anything about the situation; but then none of them were heroes; on the other hand, Radetzky thought ironically, it would have been highly improper for any of the diplomats present to behave more heroically than their host. They were probably now thanking God that the responsibility was not theirs, that they were not in their own embassies—and he knew that, no matter what their host and colleague would do, they would always feel free to criticize him later in their reports and conversations, and let it be known what they would have done had they been in charge.

The Ambassador himself was coming slowly down the red-carpeted stairs and nervous figures were lurking behind the marble balustrade on the top floor. The Ambassador was a very short, distinguished man in his early sixties, with white hair, a noble forehead and strong, pure Spanish features. His face was the color of old ivory and his dark and gentle eyes seemed to throw a shadow around them. He represented only a very small South American country, but he could trace his ancestry back to the days of the Conquistadors.

Díaz rose immediately from the chair where he had collapsed, and bowed, in the probable hope that this politeness would be noticed and remembered later.

"Gentlemen," the Ambassador said, "I must protest."

Although Almayo had never held any official position in the country, the Ambassador had always eagerly sought his company and had often entertained him as his guest of honor. But now he behaved as though he had never seen him before. Almayo felt hurt and angry, until he noticed that the Ambassador's chin and lower lip were shaking slightly, and as long as he knew that he was scared of him, that was all he wanted. Fear was the greatest and best form of respect a man could command.

"We are asking for political asylum, Your Excellency," he said, grinning. "As you have noticed perhaps, there is something like a revolution going on here and I'll have to leave the country. Now, in accordance with the tradition in such cases, we came to your Embassy to seek asylum. We ask you to intervene on our behalf and to procure for me and my political associates a safe conduct to leave this country temporarily. In the meantime, we are claiming the right to remain in your Embassy."

"You have never held any official or political position in

this country, *señor*," the Ambassador said. "The right of political asylum is not extended to criminals. I therefore must ask you to leave the premises immediately."

Almayo's grin became bigger. He was beginning to enjoy himself.

"You cannot do that, Your Excellency," he said. "It would be a black spot on your country's good name. Besides, we don't feel like dying just now. We are not quite ready."

"Life has been very good to us, Your Excellency," Radetzky said, still looking through the peephole in the door. "We cannot desert it. Life needs us, it has appreciated our efforts. We are still young, strong, full of enterprise, and life still has the right to expect a great deal from us."

"I must tell you," Almayo went on, "that the southern provinces are completely loyal to me—and the best troops are there. You cannot throw me out. Your government would not approve of it. I received a very friendly letter from your President only a few days ago."

The Ambassador bit his lip. It was true that he had been mistaken. Only two weeks ago he had assured his government in a political report that Almayo had the situation well in hand, that the opposition was strictly nonexistent and that the dictator should be shown some new mark of personal esteem.

Almayo was looking now toward the top of the stairs. A young woman in evening dress was leaning against the marble balustrade. He didn't pay much attention to her; he just didn't want to be shot at suddenly from above.

"There's nothing I can do for you," the Ambassador said. "I must ask you to leave at once."

"And be killed like dogs?" Almayo asked, displaying a pained surprise.

"I can negotiate with the Army and obtain for you the promise of a fair trial," the Ambassador said. "I am sure they would like to try you. I am quite willing to obtain the promise of the officer in charge that you will not be physically molested."

"Physically molested is a nice, diplomatic expression for it," Radetzky said.

"I don't think I can do more," the Ambassador said. "And may I ask you why you chose to ask my Embassy rather than another?"

"Your President is my friend," Almayo said. "Our two countries are on excellent terms. Who knows, maybe he will have to ask political asylum at our Embassy in your capital tomorrow? It's merely that it happened to me first, that's all."

"The President of this country is Señor Carriedo," the Ambassador said. "Not you."

"Señor Carriedo has just been hanged from the lamp post before the presidential palace," Almayo said. "Then they attached tin cans to his body and dragged it through the streets. I wish I could have seen that—such a fine man."

"I am quite prepared to inform the officer in charge that you wish to surrender peacefully," the Ambassador repeated, "that you will walk out of here unarmed. I am quite willing to discuss the matter with them and to obtain assurance of a fair trial. That much I can promise you."

"I am not crazy," Almayo said.

The Ambassador raised his voice a little, but it was shaking perceptibly. "If you refuse my offer, there is nothing left for me but to call the soldiers in," he said.

"You would do such a thing, Your Excellency?" Almayo asked. "And . . . expose the life of the young and beautiful lady upstairs—your daughter, eh? There is a strong family

candles and lights seemed to be arranged so as to add the finishing touches to the perfection of her attire.

As he sipped his glass of Burgundy pensively, looking at her, Radetzky for the first time felt a brief but sharp flash of hope and longing, but then this must have been because he was a little tired.

The conversation was full of silences, of uneasy laughter, and the men spoke with unnatural detachment, not listening to each other, but each trying to show a worldly self-control and sense of humor. Then they rose from the table and had their coffee in the drawing room. After a glass or two of brandy, the guests fell noticeably silent, or tried to find words, which sounded hollow and only seemed to bring closer the long-postponed moment that was approaching with the inevitability of a clock.

At last, the Ambassador cleared his throat and put his glass down. As the silence fell, with only the sound of the glass ringing on the marble mantelpiece, Almayo gestured quickly toward Díaz.

"And now," he said, turning toward his host, "I shall ask the permission of Your Excellency to allow one of my friends to entertain the company with his talent as a conjurer. He's not the best man in the trade, but he's willing."

For the next quarter of an hour, while the Ambassador drummed impatiently with his fingers on the mantel piece, Díaz entertained them nervously, producing a pack of cards, shuffling them uneasily, and often missing his trick, under the stony eyes of the audience. He produced lighted cigarettes from his mouth and extracted a rubber snake that wriggled in his hand from the French Ambassador's white waistcoat.

With drops of sweat glistening on his forehead, pale shaking cheeks, terrified eyes, the waxen ends of his mustache trembling at each twist of his mouth, his jet-black dyed hair falling down and sticking to his forehead, rolling his eyes from time to time toward the grinning Almayo, he performed like an obedient dog, with the props he always carried in his pocket when in his master's company.

But then, in his panic, Díaz fumbled in his routine; seizing a lighted cigarette by the wrong end, he uttered a cry of pain, while at the same time upsetting a glass, which fell to pieces at the French Ambassador's feet.

There was an embarrassed silence, and then their host said in a voice that seemed to have gained its firmness from the unlucky failure of the conjurer's trick: "I must now ask you to leave."

"Okay, okay," Almayo said in English, in a sudden display of good humor. He pulled the gun out of its holster and gestured toward the girl.

"You are coming with us. Take a few clothes; it will be a long journey."

There was a gasp from the ladies and the Ambassador moved forward a step, but only one step.

"And hurry up," Almayo said. "I give you about three minutes. Otherwise I'll shoot His Excellency and you still will have to go."

The girl hesitated a moment and walked toward the stairs, followed by Radetzky, who watched while she threw some clothes into a bag. She seemed remarkably composed, or perhaps, Radetzky thought, having always lived the sheltered existence of the privileged, happy few, she was unable to imagine herself facing any real danger. At one moment she hesitated, but it was only because she was thinking of what clothes to take. She might have been taking off for a weekend with friends. Then she took the bag and left the room, followed by Radetzky, who felt embarrassed and remorseful.

There was a noticeable change of atmosphere downstairs. The ladies were sobbing now, and the men stood, pale-faced, facing Almayo's gun. The Cujon was in white clothes and he had put his hat on to have his hands free. Surrounded by these middle-aged, distinguished-looking men in dinner jackets and ladies in evening gowns, he stood there like one of those statues dug up from the deepest recesses of the pre-Columbian past.

He instructed the Chief of Protocol to go out and warn the officers in charge that if they tried to shoot or stop them or follow them, the Ambassador's daughter, whom they were taking with them as a hostage, would be killed instantly. The parley took a few minutes and they began to move toward the door. But then Almayo had an even better idea, to ensure being covered on all sides.

For several weeks afterward, the newspapers of the world were to scream in horror and shame, denouncing the cowardly dictator who had walked out of the Embassy protected on all sides by the wives of the British, French and American Ambassadors, with a gun pointed at the back of the girl walking in front of him.

As they opened the door, they were temporarily blinded by searchlights that were converging on the house from all sides, and they knew that there were hundreds of soldiers on the neighboring houses and in the streets, with every gun pointed in their direction. There were twenty or thirty news photographers hovering on top of the Embassy walls, on top of cars, and the picture of the grinning Cujon made the front page of every newspaper all over the world.

They walked into the blinding light, and Radetzky wondered if the young officers of the revolution were idealistic enough to sacrifice the life of a young girl and two or three middle-aged ladies rather than allow the dictator to escape. He calculated that their chances of survival were in direct proportion to the degree of idealistic feelings, of education and cultural background of the commanding officers. If they were tough and resolute, completely realistic, then they would shoot all the same, and they did not have a chance. If they were full of noble feelings and respect for human decency and human life, then in all probability they would abstain from firing. He decided that this was also a test of the revolutionaries' capacity to establish themselves firmly— of their lasting power. If they refused to shoot now, just to spare a young girl's life, if they truly had this humanitarian streak of respect for life in them, then they would soon be overthrown and everything would be as it was before. A revolution that hesitates before a victim is condemned to failure.

Thus, he was deeply reassured when they reached the station wagon and stepped in without a shot being fired. The car started slowly, driven by Radetzky, first in the light, and then into darkness.

XVIII

"ANYWAY, I have done my best."

She looked triumphantly at the young evangelist. There was a silence. Dr. Horwat stared soberly at his feet. It was impossible to believe that such horrors truly existed. And yet the events of the last few hours had been quite convincing. He saw now that even in his most vocal denunciations, as he hovered with both arms outstretched like wings over the silent crowds, he had never given the enemy his due. He had lived only in America and that is why he knew very little of wickedness. It also appeared to him now that he had lacked talent and that in his most poetical and inspired flights of oratory he had never succeeded in describing the evil that ruled the earth in its true light, or rather, he quickly corrected himself, in its true darkness.

They were sitting among the rocks in some remote spot in the mountains. As the cars had come to a stop in those black lava wastes, and they were told to get out, Dr. Horwat felt certain that this was the spot chosen for their execution; but Captain García merely informed them that they were going to spend the night there, and perhaps even stay in the place longer than that—and that again seemed to carry a sinister implication. The girl was still determined to tell him everything, and often it sounded as if she were proud of herself, as if she expected some approval, or even admiration.

"Why didn't you just go home?" he asked sternly.

"I couldn't. I felt there was a challenge here—something

useful to be done, something creative. Back home, there is nothing a girl, even with a college degree, can do really, except make a living. There is nothing exceptional or great to pit yourself against. I suppose you'll think that I am presumptuous, all the time boasting, but could you tell me where else I could have achieved what I've achieved here? I've given this country the best telephone system outside the United States. It reaches everywhere and it's automatic and it has become the pride of the country. All the tourists notice it. You probably noticed it yourself; even in that café, in that cheap, dilapidated place, there was a telephone, and it worked—and Captain García obtained his connection immediately."

Dr. Horwat gave her an injured glance. That she should pride herself on what had almost cost them their lives—that awful black telephone on the counter that he would never forget as long as he lived—was something that he found profoundly shocking.

"My dear child . . ." he began.

She was not listening.

"And then, of course, I loved him. And I still love him very much. He's such a challenge, really. There's so much I can do for him. It's wonderful to feel that you can be useful, really useful, to the man you love, that you can change him, that you can help him. It makes your love truly creative. Back home, you just don't feel that men need you. I mean, the way José needs me: truly desperately. Oh, he would never admit this, of course—he has that typical Latin vanity. But I know."

Dr. Horwat shut his eyes. That this wretched girl could sincerely claim to be in love with such a man, in love the way he himself, Dr. Horwat, loved his wife, somehow seemed to throw a disreputable light on his own feelings and on love in general and even on his own wife. He wished she would leave him alone—he did not want to listen to her sordid tales. He was exhausted, bewildered, exasperated and frightened. They had been driving for hours, and then there had been the awful moment when that man García had stopped the caravan and ordered them out once more—and this time the evangelist felt certain that he would have them shot and throw their bodies over the precipice. In fact, that seemed to him to be the whole purpose of this insane drive into the Sierra: to find the proper place for murdering them and for disposing of their bodies so that they would never be found.

But Captain García had no such intention. He had merely decided that they were dangerously low on gasoline and had packed them into one car, leaving the others behind, after emptying their tanks.

And then there was that Cuban horror, who never left his side. He had obviously decided that the evangelist would protect him, and even now he was sitting on the ground barely a few feet away; Dr. Horwat didn't dare to look at him because he knew that he would immediately give him one of his repulsive smiles.

The night was almost there; the mountains were black around them but the sky was still blue.

"Look," the girl said.

Monsieur Antoine was standing on a rock, outlined against the sky, a tall dark silhouette, with his hands moving quickly up and down. Monsieur Antoine was juggling. The silvery balls flying in the air were catching small particles of red light: . . . seven, eight, nine, ten balls, the evangelist counted. A remarkable feat for human hands, but how it appeared to the millions of stars that were looking down the evangelist could only wonder.

"Not bad," a voice said next to him. The dummy was holding one arm around the ventriloquist's neck, watching the performance.

"Not bad," the dummy repeated, "but not good enough either. The sunset was much better, in my humble opinion. There's a much greater talent around us, gentlemen, and there's simply no point in trying to match it. He does his best, though."

The stars were looking down at Monsieur Antoine's futile proclamation of dignity.

"Watch him," the dummy said. "He's trying to show them what *he* can do. Megalomaniac!"

The girl laughed. The evangelist did not like the dummy —it was something almost personal, which probably had to do with its cynical grin.

"All failures," the dummy said. "Michelangelo, Shakespeare, Einstein—all bums. Mortals. No talent. It's enough to take one look at this sky to know that."

As the juggler walked back toward them, Dr. Horwat complimented him on his skill.

"I keep trying," Monsieur Antoine said. He glanced toward the soldiery. "Do you think they still plan to shoot us?"

"Quite likely," Dr. Horwat said.

"I just can't understand why even a dictator would do such a thing," Monsieur Antoine said.

"Maybe he's disillusioned with artists," the dummy quipped.

"I am not particularly afraid to die," Monsieur Antoine said. "I suppose that's part of the act, but I have a wife and three children back in Marseille."

"Well, they're safe there," the girl said.

"You are a little cynical, Mademoiselle. I can assure you

that we attach a certain value to human life in France."

He walked away. The girl laughed.

"These Frenchmen!" she said. "The way they talk about human life, you'd think they invented it. Well, we have human life in America too. In fact, the world is so full of human life that some people begin to get thoroughly sick of it."

Later that night, Dr. Horwat, who had fallen asleep in a state of complete nervous exhaustion on the ground, was awakened by something which he instantly recognized as the sound of revelry. There was a lot of laughter and cries and sounds of drunken voices.

An orgy, Dr. Horwat thought, as he sat up. He instantly glanced around to see if the girl was there. He was rather surprised to see that she was asleep, huddled against a rock.

The headlights of one of the cars were turned on, illuminating a group of drunken soldiers. Dr. Horwat felt it his duty to get up and walk toward them just to make sure that they weren't murdering someone. Then he heard the sound of a fiddle. In the bright light that tore a circle of earth out of the darkness, he saw Mr. Manulesco, standing on his head and playing Bach on his minuscule fiddle. He was still wearing his musical clown's outfit that sparkled and glittered in the light.

Captain García, perfectly drunk, was swaggering in front of him, a bottle in his hand, exhorting the artist to give his best. Captain García was having the time of his life. He now felt an intoxication with his complete freedom and with the stimulating, exhilarating fact that he had at last been able to revert to type, to become what his ancestors had always been before him: a mountain bandit.

He danced in front of the virtuoso, who must have been

standing on his head playing Bach longer than ever before in his whole virtuoso's life. Dr. Horwat had to admit that his music was not bad, and that the man was not without talent.

Then, when he collapsed on the ground at last, and sat there with the fiddle in one hand and the bow in the other, his head lowered, panting heavily and staring at the ground, Captain García looked for another artist. He noticed the Cuban boy and dragged him into the spotlight but then, as the artist said something very shyly with a guilty smile, Captain García roared with laughter and, after sharing the excellent joke with the rest of his band, patted the boy affectionately on the back and passed him the bottle.

Suddenly, his eye fell on Dr. Horwat's face, and before he knew what was happening, the young evangelist found himself dragged through the odious crowd into the blinding light. Captain García ordered him to perform and, as Dr. Horwat, in a voice shaking with indignation and anger, tried to explain to him that he was only a preacher, the captain took this as a personal offense and pulled his gun.

"Dance!" he ordered. "You dance for me!"

But Dr. Horwat was not going to dance. In fact, he was quite prepared to lose his life rather than his dignity. Not that he wasn't scared, with that drunken ape shaking his gun under his nose. He was scared. In fact, he was so scared that a most ungodly flow of insults came bursting from his mouth, and he emptied himself of his fear, exasperation and shame in one of his most thunderous performances.

He roared as he had never roared before, and the young magnificence of his voice made the mounting hills resound with a thousand echoes and, although the flow of profanities would have profoundly shocked the millions of his followers, it was nevertheless one of his most courageous and noble efforts.

What he did not realize, however, as he stood there facing the gun and giving his best, was that Captain García had actually succeeded in his purpose and made him give a performance. All he knew, in his rage and indignation, was that his bellowing voice was shaking the mountains; somehow, while still roaring, he began to notice this and to listen to the echoes with a certain amount of satisfaction. This calmed him considerably, and he stopped to catch his breath.

"Muy bien," Captain García said, smacking his lips. "Very good. Plenty talent."

He passed the bottle to Dr. Horwat, and, although he could not quite believe it later, the young evangelist found himself having rather a large gulp of some mighty liquor.

He then staggered back into the night and was quite relieved to see the girl still asleep against the rock. Feeling as if he were coming home, he settled himself as well as he could on the ground next to her and, though his heart was still pounding with fury and his forehead covered with sweat and his mind still full of new and even more scathing words that were composing themselves into easily rolling phrases, after a few heavy sighs and a little muttering, the young evangelist sank into a merciful slumber.

XIX

THE STARS were in full bloom: the night is good for them, Almayo thought, just as the day is good for the crops. He lay on his back among the rocks, gazing up at them. The stars, that's where the old gods had come from, many thousands of years ago. They had come from the sky, and had ruled the people for a long, long time—but then the Spaniards had come from the earth and had destroyed the old gods; they had brought their own and greater God and devil with them, who were much more powerful. The ruins of the old gods were lying about all over the land, but they were nothing but petrified stones now, and had lost all their magic power. The people no longer believed in them, because they had been beaten, because they had lost to the new God and to the devil. They accepted the new belief because it had proved its power. Almayo always looked at the sky with deep respect—that's where the true talent was.

There were the twisted shadows of cacti above him, and strange-shaped rocks that sometimes seemed to move and come to life. But this was only an illusion, for the earth belonged to men. His friends had often called him "the star-eater." It was the name they gave in the tropical valleys of his birth to those who were mastala addicts. It gave them great happiness and permitted them to see God in their visions. But they called him that only jokingly, not because he ate the plant, which only good enough for old peasants like his mother, but because of the hundreds of stars who had appeared in his night club, because of his constant search for greater and better talent; it was, they said, as if he were devouring them all, and still looking for more. Everybody needed magic to stay alive. It just so happened that he needed it more than anyone else.

Now he was on the run in the Sierra, with only a few friends and the hope that there was still some luck left with him, that in the southern peninsula the troops under General Ramón were still loyal. Perhaps he would never see his night club again. Then he would have to make do only with those distant stars shining in the sky, with their constant and never-fulfilled promise of mystery and magic. It was possible that those millions of lights in the heavens, too, were nothing but fakes and cheats, and that they had no more to offer than all those other little fakes and cheats he had seen on the floor of his club.

Yet he knew that somewhere in this world there was a friend waiting for him, a fabulous being whose unique powers were beyond dispute, and whose identity had long been evident to him. Thousands of people had seen him, and it was just his bad luck that he had never been able to see him himself with his own eyes. Perhaps he was teasing him; or perhaps he still wanted to find out what he could do, how far he would go, what price he was willing to pay. The answer was any price, except that he had paid it already, that he had given everything he had in him, and so it was now or never. In a few days, in a few hours, it might well be too late. But perhaps that was the price he had to pay to see him with his own eyes: to die. He was quite willing and not afraid. It was a little strange that he should be asked to go so far when others had paid just the usual and much cheaper price of admission of viciousness and shame.

It was enough for him to think of that fellow "Jack" and

of his assistant to feel an overwhelming frustration and despair and to almost cry with rage. It was wrong that he, Almayo, of all people should never have been allowed to meet him. He had shown himself worthy—a thousand times—he had scrupulously committed every sin the priests had described to him as sure to please Him who ruled the wicked earth; the only possible explanation was that this fellow "Jack," or rather his assistant, or both, were teasing him, that they enjoyed torturing him and this, perhaps, was also part of the price he had to pay.

For more than ten years now, he had been offered nothing but cheap circus trash, even if they called themselves true artists, and now, when the real thing came, it seemed to elude him, it almost looked as if it were too late.

Even so, they had been fortunate in their escape, and he was not without hope. They had met some remnants of the Security Force on the outskirts of the city and had dashed toward the Sierra, with machine guns blazing at the first sign of hostility or even of life. They had driven on for as long as the road lasted into the mountains and then they had found horses and a guide to show them the way. The guide swore that he would lead them across, that it would take them no more than two days on horseback to reach the southern slopes and the first military outpost of General Ramón.

They could have tried the road that linked the capital directly with the city of Gombaz, in the south, and some of the men had decided to take that chance and risk the three-hundred-mile drive along the open road. If their luck held, they could reach General Ramón in less than four hours, and then the helicopter would be despatched to pick up Almayo on the Sierra trail. Things could still come out all right, and as he lay there listening to the silence, looking at the silhouettes of the guards on the edge of the precipice—there was no danger around, only the friendly night—he felt a new confidence, a new strength in his body, a new faith in the glittering stars. It would be plain bad luck if some of his men didn't get across, and his luck was still good. He was far from beaten. Tomorrow morning, the helicopter would come to pick them up. It would come down from the sky slowly, just as that fellow "Jack" did in his act. He still wished dreamily that he could see him with his own eyes, talk to him, tell him everything he had done to deserve his attention, and even as he fell asleep, he still felt in his heart a torturing, devouring thirst for talent.

XX

THEY HAD BEEN on the road once more since dawn, all in
one car now, since Captain García had decided that, even
so, he had barely enough gasoline to reach his destination.
They were so tightly packed and the heat was such that
Dr. Horwat was at times half-conscious, and these were
moments of relief, for when his senses returned to him, the
bounces of the car over the dirt road, the sight of the
precipice barely a few feet away, the physical contact of the
Cuban, who practically held him in his arms, the blank stare
of the dummy leaning over the shoulder of Agge Olsen,
who sat in front of him, the livid, sweat-covered faces of
his companions, and the suffocating smell of overheated
steel were more than he could stand; it was like sitting in
the center of the devil's grin; and he had indeed felt certain
during his whole adventure that he was the object of his
enemy's personal attention.

"Cheer up, Dr. Horwat," the dummy croaked. "It won't
be long now."

And there was no denying the sinister threat of that
remark, for it had been their bad luck that Captain García
had sobered up enough during the early hours of the
morning to tune in his service radio; he had learned that
the capital had fallen and that the "bloodthirsty, murderous
thief, José Almayo," had vanished; but then, listening to
the southern command, he was informed that the port city
of Gombaz, under General Ramón, was still loyal and determined to march on the capital to reinstate order. And
so Captain García had decided to make a dash toward

Gombaz; it was the only possible escape door toward some friendly shore. There, he announced to his prisoners, they would be delivered to the proper authorities and their fate decided—and everything would depend, he added with a friendly wink, on the whereabouts of General Almayo. Some of them saw in this new turn of events a reason for hope; Dr. Horwat knew better, and he felt a little irritated by his companions' sudden burst of optimism, in which he merely saw a pathetic and somewhat cowardly sign of wishful thinking. He knew that he was now paying the price of all his past victorious rounds against his enemy, for the past successes of his spiritual crusade. Humiliated, badly mauled and forced into retreat, the evil spirit had cunningly and treacherously lured him into this country, which was his personal kingdom, and on this familiar ground was submitting him now to a merciless punishment.

"I don't believe we will get out of this alive," he declared, crossing his arms on his chest for, sitting tightly pressed between the Cuban monster and the girl, there was nowhere else he could put them. "The devil will see to it."

"Here he goes again," the girl said, shaking her head sadly. "You really should know better, Dr. Horwat. It is, of course, a nice figure of speech, but you know perfectly well that the devil doesn't exist, that he's a figment of popular imagination."

"What is the matter now, preacher?" the dummy asked. "You look as if you'd suffered a personal loss."

Dr. Horwat didn't bother to answer. He just glared at the loathsome thing.

"No, sir, you are entirely wrong there," the dummy remarked. "I may be only a dummy, but I'm not an atheist. I believe in the Supreme Ventriloquist. All of us puppets do."

Dr. Horwat closed his eyes.

XXI

THE VALLEY was emerging from shadows; the gray rocks
and silvery-green shrubs of the Sierra Dolores were rising
slowly toward the paling sky, but the light was not yet able
to reach all the narrow recesses of the earth. There was
almost no path and what was left of the confusing, twisting
trail looked at each turn as if it were going to end at the
next stone. The horses were unaccustomed to the high
altitude and once more they had to dismount and rest
them.

The Spanish girl was looking toward the rising sun and
it was quite possible, Radetzky thought, that she was enjoying the sight and thought of nothing else. Never, since they
had left the Embassy, had she shown any sign of anxiety or
panic. He had expected her to become hysterical, to cry, to
implore, but she remained silent and composed. During
their last halt, she had slept quite peacefully on the ground,
and she had never complained. Perhaps she was merely
stunned, or else there was some deep inner confidence that
sustained her. She wore a little gold cross on a chain around
her neck and maybe she believed in God. He could see her
profile against the sky. With her dark hair touched by the
morning light, she seemed not only beautiful but almost
happy. It was as if her own youth and that of the rising sun
had established some reassuring alliance. She looked mysterious and as this thought occurred to him Radetzky shook
his head at his own naïveté. There was no mystery on
earth. And yet he hardly dared to speak to her; even a few

words could destroy an illusion. The mystery of a woman's face was nothing but craving in a man's heart; another make-believe, a good performance, a clever veil thrown over some humble and mortal insignificance; an act not very different from that of any good traveling magician.

There was nothing more in the mystery of the Giaconda smile than the clever stroke of a brush, nothing but the hand of a good performing artist. He knew—and yet he still kept looking, watching the strangeness of that face as if it had something to offer. It was not enough to know; the hope would always be there and the craving.

He also knew that Díaz, who lay asleep on the ground, was only a charlatan; that he was betraying Almayo and reporting to his enemies on his slightest move. He knew that the Baron was probably nothing but a drunk, and that his air of almost metaphysical mystery and remoteness hid nothing deeper than a pocket flask. Above all, he knew about himself, Leif Bergstrom, a Swedish journalist, who had played as well and as recklessly as he could the part of Otto Radetzky, to get close to the dictator and write the story of a true believer.

He had set himself a dangerous task and he had succeeded only too well. It was doubtful that he would live to write his story. To get it, he had come as close as a human being can to selling his soul to the devil, and it was quite likely that he was now going to pay the price. The only man who knew the truth was the Swedish Consul and he had warned him repeatedly that there would be very little that he could do for him in case of trouble.

He had played his part well, and he had been helped by his physique, the flat, impudent face with pale blue eyes, with typical German scars across one cheek—due, not to dueling, but to an automobile accident. He had the appearance, the air, the aura of a free adventurer, of Otto Radetzky, the soldier of fortune, one of Hitler's most trusted paratroop officers, the arms smuggler, the daredevil —and he had managed to pull off his trick and to cheat José Almayo. He had an ideal physique for that; it had always been enough for him to enter any military head-quarters in the Middle East, for instance, to be taken imme-diately for granted.

They had six soldiers with them, and two of Almayo's personal guards, and they were watching the rocks for any sign of danger; they were now in Raphael Gómez country. It was doubtful if the helicopter would find them in this chaos of rocks and it was even more doubtful that any of the messengers had managed to reach the southern head-quarters. At least they were safe from pursuit. He opened his map and checked once more, but no road reached there, and the only highway to Gombaz made a large loop around the Sierra.

The Baron sat on a rock completely unperturbed. With some help from his pocket flask, he could preserve the feel-ing of superiority which reduced history, the world's great-est events and whatever happened to himself to insignifi-cant little waves lapping at his feet. His clothes were a little rumpled now, but he still managed to keep an air of personal distinction, and his attitude of nonviolent resistance, his absolute refusal to have anything to do with the human situation in these prehistoric years. It was not that he nourished a secret hope that the divine powers that had presided over creation, and still, presumably, watched over the evolution of living things, would take notice of his in-dignant, if silent, protest. It was merely a matter of personal dignity, almost of personal hygiene. For the last twenty-five years he had been a resolute nonpartisan—a conscien-

tious objector, who protested against the biological, intellectual and physical limitations imposed upon mankind.
He came from a very noble and ancient family, the tribe
of indestructible idealists, and he was implacably, if pas-
sively, refusing to accept, to share, to submit.

He allowed himself to be thrown from one adventure to
another, floating like some unsinkable cork above everything that befell him. There was nothing that could surprise him, not even José Almayo; he was but a timid soul
compared to a certain German dictator who had extermin-
ated six million people in gas chambers for the sake of an
ideological superstition that was no less primitive than that
of that Cujon dreamer, but merely expressed in contemporary jargon.

The Indian girl sat silently on the ground. She had remained unconcerned throughout the journey; she had always been a camp follower and she did not seem unduly
perturbed or upset. It was only when she caught her nylon
stockings against a rock or when she tore the sleeve of her
American jacket that she began to swear and to scream at
Almayo, trying to scratch his face. He held her laughingly
and, at the last halt, he had taken her without even bother-
ing to get out of sight.

Then he had winked at Radetzky and, pointing to the
Spanish girl, had asked: "Why don't you have her?"

"It would be bad manners," Radetzky told him.

A little later, he noticed that Almayo was talking to Díaz,
grinning and pointing to the girl. He took a rifle from one
of the soldiers, and told him: "I'll see if I can shoot something to eat."

He started to climb among the rocks. After a few
minutes, he was over the first ridge and, looking down, he
saw Díaz walking slowly toward the girl. He saw Díaz take

the girl by the hand and walk with her along the path and out of sight. Radetzky climbed down a little and rounded some rocks, and saw Díaz again, walking with the girl, holding her hand and obviously searching for a place. He kept looking back fearfully from time to time to see if Almayo was out of sight. Then he pushed the girl behind a rock. Radetzky lifted his rifle and took good aim—but then he smiled, and lowered his weapon. He could clearly see Díaz taking a pack of cards from his pocket and, standing in front of the girl, with obvious nervousness and embarrassment, perform some of his tricks. Radetzky laughed. He should have known; these were the only tricks the old boy still knew how to perform. He climbed down the path and handed the rifle back to the soldier.

It was then that they heard the helicopter for the first time. It had appeared from behind the mountain and it began to move in their direction, although it was doubtful if they had been seen yet. The messengers had managed to reach General Ramón, after all. It was an Army helicopter and they could now read the white number of the regiment on its side. The soldiers fired into the air to attract the attention of the crew. Almayo was at once on his feet, a figure in white, grinning broadly and waving his hat. The helicopter made a sharp turn and plunged toward them; they had been seen. It was hovering not more than thirty feet above their heads and they could easily see the pilot and the officers behind them.

Then, suddenly, it came: a sharp burst of machine gun fire, the whining of bullets, the jumping dust among the rocks. Almayo stood absolutely still with his hat raised high in his hand, as if he were saluting, and then he looked at the white sleeve of his left arm where blood was beginning to appear. He retreated slowly behind a rock. For an endless moment, the helicopter hovered over them, spraying them with bullets. Two of the soldiers had been killed, but the others were now returning the fire. Then the helicopter rose almost vertically and was gone. The Indian girl was lying crumpled behind a rock. It was obvious that both her American clothes and herself were damaged beyond recovery. She did not complain or cry and her face had the centuries-old expression of acceptance of her race. She died with her eyes open, staring calmly ahead.

They still had nine hours of daylight left and there was nowhere they could hide and nothing they could do but follow the narrow trail. It was certain that the helicopter would soon return. Two of the horses had been wounded and had to be shot.

Their guide had disappeared; they saw him take one big jump among the rocks, and then he had vanished. They proceeded on their way once more, watching the sky.

Almayo's left arm had two bullets in it and it was a bad wound; Radetzky knew it would begin to fester within the hour. Then they began to hear the engine again, and scattered immediately, watching for the helicopter to reappear, but the sky remained empty and the engine went on and on, and then receded into the distance. It came from somewhere on the other side of the mountain ridge, but the pilot knew where they were now and it was strange that he had missed them. They went on for more than two hours and then again the noise of the engine came clearly, this time from close by. They stopped once more and listened. Radetzky could hardly believe his ears.

"Cars," he said.

"You crazy?" Almayo shouted. "There's no road here. Look at the map. It's a good map. The Army printed it only last year."

Radetzky checked the map once more. It was true; there was no road there. It must have been the helicopter looking for them on the wrong side of the ridge. Then they heard the cars again, quite close, and this time it was the unmistakable sound of gears, brakes and tires. They followed the path to the top of a ridge, a hundred yards ahead of them, and stared in silence. There was a road there, a dirt road, and there were traces of tires on it.

"The American bitch," Almayo exclaimed in despair, stamping his cigar into the ground. She had managed to convince him to build some new roads; they were going to bring civilization to the distant villages and improve the lot of the peasants. The Army and the police had approved the idea. It was the best way to control the population, and so he had built the new roads, just as he had built the telephone system, to put the whole country within his easy reach, and here was one of the roads, too recent to have been marked on the map.

They were now at the mercy of military patrols. Almayo knew that only a miracle could save him. As they moved higher up along the path and above the road, he pulled his horse back, his mouth gaped, his eyes froze and perhaps for the only time in his life he felt truly scared, and he spat on the ground in superstitious terror.

For the first thing he saw was the American girl, sitting on a stone behind a black Cadillac, writing something in a notebook held on her knee. She had her glasses on and she was completely absorbed in her letter.

XXII

IN HIS PHYSICAL PAIN and exhaustion from loss of blood, and with the fever already hammering at his temples, he thought at first that he was seeing a ghost. It could not be; she was dead. He had given the order to one of his most trusted officers and no one had ever dared to disobey his orders.

But then he saw other human figures pressed together inside the Cadillac and the two military jeeps, and soldiers standing there talking, and an officer, who was pressing a bottle to his lips, and he recognized the face of Captain García at once. His orders had not been carried out; and this shook him more than anything else he had experienced during the last few hours. In his rage, he spurred his horse and it almost jumped from the rock into the chasm, and then backed away, neighing, for it knew more of fear than its rider. Almayo dismounted, swearing through his clenched teeth, and rounded the rock, to appear suddenly above the road, outlined against the sky. They saw him.

They stared at him in silence and Captain García, who was still drinking, slowly brought the bottle down and stared longer than the others, for he knew now that as far as he was concerned this was the end of the journey. He threw the bottle away, wiped his mouth and, as Almayo climbed down and walked slowly toward him, he stood at attention and saluted. He wanted to tell him that he had tried to reach the city of Gombaz—it lay only a few hundred feet below them—but then had learned from his radio that the garrison there had rebelled and had sided with his enemies, but he remained silent, standing at attention, waiting for the orders to come.

It was then that the American girl, raising her eyes from the letter she was writing, caught sight of Almayo, and with an exclamation of joy, her face flushed with delight, she ran toward him. Then she saw that he was badly wounded, and that his face was pale with exhaustion and despair.

"Oh, my poor darling," she exclaimed. "What have they done to you?"

He cursed and pushed her away, and gave García his orders. The Captain shouted to his men and they rushed toward the car, dragging the prisoners out and lining them up on the side of the road against the rocks. García ordered the firing squad into position and they raised and cocked their weapons, and then, still disbelieving that he had himself been spared, the Captain gave the first command.

But Almayo stopped him. He pointed his finger to the prisoners lined up against the rocks, and told him: "You go with them. You are going to die with them—and you will give the command."

García obeyed at once. He gave Almayo one gloomy look, and it was as close as he had ever dared to come to defying him; then he took his place at the end of the line, pushed his cap back and barked the first order. It was his turn to be robbed. The gold of life was being taken away from him; it would fill the pockets of those who would live on. And he was grateful that the ancient custom of the land, the favor given to officers to command their own execution, had been granted to him, for it filled him with that exaltation and intoxication of drama and self-importance that made death easier to swallow. He was now eager to live it up, to live up his death to the utmost, but he had to wait, for Almayo was passing slowly before the prisoners, looking into their faces.

Dr. Horwat was facing the firing squad with an expression of dignity and scorn that would have made his poor wife cry with pride and joy, if only he could have shown her a snapshot. He was thanking God for the end of his predicament; the thought occurred to him that this was certainly the most un-American thing that had ever happened on this earth, but then he remembered the Crucifixion and knew how close he had come to blasphemy in his last thoughts.

"Why do you do this, José?" Charlie Kuhn asked.

"You just leave that to me, Charlie," Almayo said. "This man Raphael Gómez won't get away with it, eh? No one ever dared to shoot American citizens before. But he dares. Who is this fellow?"

He was looking at the Cuban boy.

"The world's one and only true superman," Charlie said, and Almayo laughed.

He pointed a finger at the evangelist.

"Nothing personal," he said. "Just politics. It's difficult to get power and it's difficult to keep it. You are a good man and I like what you say about the devil—you always found the best words."

"I can see him now with my own eyes," the evangelist said.

"Oh, no, you can't," Almayo said gravely. "All you can see is a man. Just a man who is trying harder than the others."

He was facing his mother now and grinned; she didn't even recognize him. She stood there chewing like an old cow and shaking with laughter. He knew that the expensive

American bag he had given her was full of mastala leaves. He had heard of no one, even among the most famous politicians of the land, among all the great of the earth, who had dared to have his own mother shot. Even the Liberator himself hadn't done it. It was certainly the worst sin— the best proof of willingness—the worst thing one could do. He felt better and his grin became bigger; he looked at his mother almost with gratitude. She was doing a lot for him.

He moved to Mr. Sheldon, the lawyer, and pointed his finger at him.

"You know," he said, "you brought me bad luck. I shouldn't have gone into legitimate business. You are honest. I shouldn't have touched honesty in any way, even with my gloves on. Maybe you ruined me."

He barely glanced at Monsieur Antoine the juggler, who stood there proudly in his shirt sleeves and braces, carrying his coat neatly folded over his arm. Monsieur Antoine didn't know why he was going to die, so he decided that he was going to die for France, and it made him feel better.

Then there was the ventriloquist with the dummy in his arms—the dummy stared at him and looked scared—and the musical clown in his costume and with his miniature fiddle—cheap circus trash, he knew them all. He tried to avoid looking at the girl. But she had left the line and faced him, and he turned his eyes away quickly. He was scared of the goodness in her.

"You go back there," he told her without looking at her.

"José, please do realize you are sick," she begged. "You need medical care, therapy, attention. You must go to the States with me, seek proper psychological help. I am sure even your political enemies will understand that. They will let you go."

Almayo cursed and turned away. Radetzky had come up

to him and was pleading angrily. He shouted to him that his hope of pinning down this murder to the new regime of Raphael Gómez was hopeless now; it was too late for the scheme to be carried out; there were too many witnesses; the new leaders would have no difficulty in establishing the truth. But the Cujon told him calmly: "Okay, okay, but I am going to do it all the same, just for luck."

It was Charlie Kuhn who saved them. For the last few minutes he had been waiting for the propitious moment, watching Almayo's face for every sign of mounting despair, pain and fever. The Cujon was half-crazed now, and it was clear that he had lost much blood. Those were the moments when a man would cling even to a smallest straw of hope.

Charlie stepped forward.

"Before you do it, José, I just want you to know why I've come to see you. I've got news for you. I've got him for you this time, José."

He didn't have to say the name. Almayo knew instantly. Charlie Kuhn saw the old, familiar spark in his eye; the eager, thirsty look of the talent scout, of the seeker.

"Perhaps you think I'm lying," Charlie Kuhn said. "Here's the cable I received three days ago. He's right here, in Gombaz, at the Hotel Flores."

He took the cable from his pocket and handed it to him. But Almayo didn't take it. He knew it was true. He had always known that one day the one and truly great, all-powerful artist would come his way. It was only natural that he should have turned up at this small city of Gombaz, when only a miracle could save him. He had very little strength left, and the world was dancing and floating around him; he would have given up long ago if his faith had not supported him.

"Hotel Flores," he heard someone say, and then he saw

a finger pointing down to the steaming town below.

Radetzky knew that he was looking at Almayo's face for the last time, and he also knew that this was how he was going to remember it for as long as he lived: with that expression of childish pleasure, expectation and wonder. He remained one brief moment turned toward the town, as if its sight conveyed to him some secret message of total reassurance; then Almayo walked toward the car and his guards and Captain García himself pleaded with him and begged him not to commit this folly. They told him that the town was now in the hands of his enemies; that if he entered it by the road, in this car, he would be immediately recognized and seized. If some important and decisive matter urged him to take such an incredible risk, he should follow the mountain path and try to sneak into the town unobserved.

He listened absent-mindedly, his eyes still fixed, as if in some happy trance, to the white walls and flat roofs below them. Then, in one swift jump, he left the road and was gone.

His two bodyguards followed him, although he had given no order, like well-trained dogs who do not have to wait for a whistle. Then, to Radetzky's surprise, he saw a black shadow follow him down the difficult and abrupt track; it was Díaz. He could hardly believe his eyes, for the last thing he expected from that creature was such loyalty and courage.

It was then that there rose from the road a loud, hoarse bark and the glitter of arms, and Dr. Horwat turned his pale and hollowed face toward it: Captain García was rapturously executing himself.

He knew that this was his last chance to make a pleasant exit; Almayo had lost and there was now no power on earth that could save his faithful servant. He would suffer the supreme dishonor, the shameful death of those who didn't know how to die: tortured, burned alive and then dragged through the streets among jeers and under the approving eyes of the populace, with tin cans attached to his body; their deafening and familiar din would bring new thousands to the windows and on the balconies for it meant the fall of a tyrant and the birth of another, and not even a dog would dare to approach his carcass. He was in just the proper state of drunken elation, laughing despair, fury, and frustrated rage and intoxication with this supreme moment of his last fiesta, and he raised his hand to announce the kill and shouted the command; his cap flew into the air and fell to the ground and then his body followed it.

"Good heavens," the dummy Ole Jensen said to his pale-faced master. "He was an artist too, after all. A real talent, my dear."

There was the sound of an engine starting and the screaming of tires and the dummy turned its head quickly toward the top of the road; the American girl had jumped behind the Cadillac's wheel, and the car was now plunging down the dirt road like a giant black insect raising his two wings of dust.

"There she goes," the dummy sighed. "What is she trying to do?"

"Maybe she thinks she can save him," the ventriloquist said.

"Hmmm," the dummy grunted. "I have yet to hear of any of you poor living things who ever managed to be saved on this earth."

"She's one of those well-meaning, determined Americans," Agge Olsen said. "And maybe she loves him. Those things do happen."

The dummy watched the clouds of dust below, then shook his head.

"Hmmm," he grunted again, this time with some trace of emotion in his voice. "Well, all I can say is this: I'm happy that I'm not human."

XXIII

HE WAS STAGGERING down the stony path and on his lips there was a smile not much different from all those smiles that live briefly on human lips when from the vastness of indifference that seems to surround them there comes a sign that they are not ignored, that they are not alone. The left side of his body was one throbbing pain, and the thorns and rocks were tearing at his flesh; the white town danced under his eyes and often almost vanished, and then he had to stop and wait for the world to return. But as he emerged from the chaos of cacti and rocks into the first cobbled street with the shopkeepers straddling their chairs in front of their stores and women rushing out to grab their children as he passed by, his spirits were high and he felt almost like singing. They recognized him and stared at him with scared faces, and they didn't believe their eyes. A badly frightened barber who had imprudently rushed out still holding a razor in his hand, barely managed to find his voice when Almayo asked him where the Hotel Flores was. He merely pointed with his razor, eager to see him move holding a razor in his hand barely managed to find his wife and children.

"Take me there."

The barber's face showed an almost frantic anguish, but he started to walk, with glazed eyes, staring ahead of him as if in a trance. He led him to the hotel, pointed to the door, and, as Almayo walked in, retreated backward, bumping against a Tommy gun in the hands of one of Almayo's guards; he jumped frantically away and started to run, but then, finding himself miraculously alive, his curiosity became suddenly greater than his fear and, with something that was to be unanimously recognized later as a supreme boldness, he just stood there, looking on, for this was one thing in his life that he would be able to talk about to his customers forever and gain fame.

Almayo stepped into the lobby with its usual chained parrot on a perch behind the cashier's desk; there was a bar to the right, with another entrance leading into the street. A few scared peasants stood staring at him.

He went quickly to the bar and ordered a drink, and then another, then grabbed the bottle and drank as long as his breath lasted. As he was putting the bottle down he saw a framed picture of himself above the café owner's head —either they hadn't had the time to take it down or perhaps they weren't so sure yet—and from the man's petrified stance and bulging eyes he knew that he had recognized him. He tried to ask his question, but felt suddenly so terrified that perhaps the El Señor had shrugged him off and left town and had gone elsewhere on his search for talent, that he barely managed to utter in a hoarse voice: "Jack."

The café owner's eyes bulged even more and he stood silent in a state of paralyzed stupor.

With his good hand, Almayo grabbed him by the shirt and shook him.

"Speak, you ass. Señor Jack, he's staying here. What room? Where is he?"

The café owner, through a haze of astonishment and fear, managed to understand that the great General Almayo, incredible as it might be, was asking him for the room number of an *artista* who was staying at the hotel with his assistant, and who was performing every night in the one and only night club in the town. Finally, finding his voice, he gasped: "Third floor, room eleven," and, as Almayo's hand left his throat, he watched him stagger into the lobby and upstairs and then grabbed the bottle and gulped all the liquor his mouth and throat could absorb, before he even began to think again.

Almayo climbed the stairs and stood a moment at the door staring at the number eleven in black enameled letters before him. His fever and the drink and the blind, crazed hope that throbbed in him with each beating of the heart were making the whole world whirl around him, and the number eleven floated in five or six different directions and above five doorknobs. Then he grabbed one of them and pushed the door open. There was a silence. He stepped in.

The world was still revolving around him, but he mastered enough strength and anger to order it to stand still. The first thing he saw was a little man in a crumpled suit, sitting on a chair. He had a yellow complexion and as Almayo looked eagerly at every detail of his face, he saw that the whites of his eyes were yellow too, and his unkempt hair was greasy just like his face, and that he watched him with an expression of mocking scorn. And then he saw something else: the man was holding a box of kitchen matches in his lap, and one of them had just finished burning in his hand; he pressed the match to his nostril and, while watching Almayo, inhaled the smell of sulfur with an obvious relish and then sighed with something like sadness or nostalgia.

"A most disreputable town and a most deplorable hotel," he said in English. "Drunken Indians everywhere. But you don't care, Jack, I know. You don't care about anything any more. You gave up. You gave up long ago. You have stopped trying. You are a has-been. You just snooze—you would snooze through anything. A pity, my dear sir, although I bet you don't understand a word of English. A thousand pities. This was a great talent—the greatest."

There was a bed to the right next to the window, and "this" was lying on the bed with a newspaper over his face. All Almayo could see was his legs in black trousers and the worn-out soles of his shoes. He could hear the man snore and he could see the newspaper move over his nose and mouth. Then the man groaned and moved slightly, but his face was still invisible. All Almayo could see was the white hair on the back of his head.

"Yes," the other fellow said moodily, "those were the days. We have known some greatness in the past, but all we have now are memories."

He took another match from the box and lit it and then after a second blew it out and immediately inhaled it with deep satisfaction.

"Yes, my dear sir, only memories and nostalgia, I may add. Decline and fall of practically everybody, as the other fellow says. Very little talent left—hardly enough to scratch out a living. But you, my dear man, you are just drunk and you don't care, and you are not acquainted with the King's English."

"I speak English," Almayo said.

The man raised his eyebrows in mild surprise.

"You do? And what are you doing here, violating our privacy—the sacred right of every Englishman? Who are you, anyway?"

"I am José Almayo," the Cujon said.

There were moments when he saw six or seven little men dancing in circles around him, and he felt faint with the loss of blood, and with longing, but there was something strange about the man, and this was already reassuring.

"José Almayo," he repeated.

The fellow lit another match and there were suddenly dozens of little lights dancing around Almayo.

"Never heard of it," the man said.

He waited for the match to burn out and then brought it to his nose, sticking it almost into his nostrils, and inhaled it.

"Splendid memories of things past—of some truly delightful places," he said.

Almayo once more summoned all his strength and stopped the world circling around him and made it stand still.

"Listen," he said. "You know who I am. I am sure you've heard about me. I . . . I am in trouble."

The man looked interested.

"Do you hear that, Jack? The man is in trouble. Now, that is something new, here below, eh? Did you hear that, Jack? Come on, wake up. You've had enough oblivion for today. Come on, face yourself, my friend."

There was a murmur from the bed and the man pushed the newspaper away. For one moment he lay there half-conscious, staring ahead. He was an old, noble-looking man, Almayo thought reverently, and he had an impressive face, with strong, good features, the hair very white. He had a short Spanish beard. His tie was undone and he was wearing a black silk waistcoat. He lifted himself warily on one elbow and stared at Almayo. He looked sad and unhappy and hurt.

"What is this?" he asked. "Who is this man? Why can't I forget this bloody world for a moment? Why is it that I am never left in peace? Who is this crazy-looking Indian?"

Almayo didn't answer. He was still clinging to hope, but

despair was so close and so quick in its merciless approach that he had to summon all his courage and all his faith to persist.

"I have heard about you," he said in a hoarse, low voice. "I have been hearing about you for years. They say you are the greatest. I believe it."

"Do you hear that, Jack?" the little man said. "He believes in us. He thinks we are the greatest."

"If anyone in this place can claim any title to greatness, it's I and I alone," Jack said.

It was obvious that he was pleased by Almayo's words. He was now sitting on his bed, passing his fingers through his noble, snow-white hair.

"Well, young man," the other fellow said, "it's nice to know that you have heard so much about us. Very nice, indeed. This fellow Jack is still a good artist, although, let's admit it, he's no longer what he used to be. Neither am I, for that matter. Sitting here, smelling these balmy sulfurous matches, instead of the real thing, just for old memories' sake. There has been a certain loss of power, a decline, it's no good denying it."

"Nobody is denying it," the old man said, shaking his head. "We all go to the dogs sooner or later."

"But we were great artists in our day, we were, and although very few remember it, some are still talking in wonder. And our friend, Jack here, was the greatest of us all. Now, young man, maybe you won't believe me, but he was able to make the sun stand still and the earth tremble, and he could make a flood—he was particularly good at floods—and a plague, although the plague was rather my department, if I may say so without sounding unduly pretentious. But we can still perform one trick or two, and if you come tonight to watch our performance, you'll see."

"Nothing to it at all," the old man mumbled. "Nothing compared to the old days—but then, of course, the new generation is less credulous, more cynical, they don't have it in them to believe in you, and so everything is becoming more and more difficult for true artists. It's very sad."

"Now, we don't want you to start crying again, Jack," the other man said. "You'll break that young man's heart. So what? So you are a has-been."

"Don't you dare call me a has-been," Jack thundered at him, throwing him a crushing glance. "Where would you be without me?"

"And where would you be without me?" the little man asked.

"I don't know at all why I am associating with you," Jack said.

"Well try to remember how it all started," the little man said mockingly. "We have always been partners. We need each other. A perfect team. Without me you wouldn't be able to make a penny. I'm part of the show, remember. True enough, you hold the spotlight, but I'm the chap who is doing all the dirty work." He stopped suddenly and stared, completely petrified, into the muzzle of the gun in Almayo's hand.

"Come on," the Cujon said. "I want to see it. I want to see it with my own eyes."

"The fellow is getting nasty," the little man said, stirring uneasily in his chair. "Why don't you come to the club tonight?"

"I have very little time left," Almayo said quietly. "Show me what you can do. I want to know. I want to see it with my own eyes. Hurry up, or I will shoot you, both of you."

"My dear Jack, this young man seems to have heard a lot of very flattering things about us," the fellow said. "I'm afraid he's asking too much for poor little traveling magicians. I suggest that you do something for him. I think it would be wise—it would be prudent, judging from his looks."

"Why is it that I am never left in peace?" Jack asked.

"Well, it seems that you still have a certain reputation," his assistant said. "This is the price of fame."

"I am not in the mood to do anything," Jack said, sitting on the bed, his head lowered.

"You have got to make a living just like everybody else," his assistant said. "The good old days of glory are gone. I even believe that if this young man puts a bullet through your heart, as he seems quite capable of doing, you will actually die, Jack. Unbelievable as it may seem."

"All right, all right," Jack grumbled.

He got up with a sigh and looked into Almayo's eyes. The Cujon was burning with fever and he had had too much to drink, and he was crazed with anguish and hope. He stood there with the gun in his hand, desperately wanting to believe, to see. Somewhere in his subconscious mind, he was even willing to be cheated. But he had seen too many tricks, he had seen all the talent they had to offer, he knew all the ropes, and even though he was exhausted and half-conscious, there was still enough in him of knowledge to make him, almost in spite of himself, resist a hypnotist's eye.

"Look," Jack said. "Watch it carefully. . . . Now, you'll see what I can do. Now you see me rising into the air and floating in space. . . ."

But all Almayo could see was an old man standing there in his socks, beating the air with his arms in the middle of a cheap hotel room, and a circus barker sitting in a chair, inhaling the sulfurous odor of burned-out matches.

"Here I am," the old man said solemnly. "Rising slowly, floating in mid-air . . . higher . . . and higher. . . . Isn't this wonderful? Isn't this a miraculous, a supernatural sight?"

He stood on the floor with his pot belly visible inside the undone trousers, his arms outstretched, looking deep into Almayo's eyes.

"And, mind you, this is nothing compared to what the old man used to do in his great days," the assistant said. "He was the greatest. He was loved and revered and admired, and all the crowned heads of Europe bowed in deep respect before him. But now he can barely rise a few feet above the ground."

"Now, you see me coming down slowly," the old man said. "There, I am back on the ground. You have seen it all."

"And perhaps, for this private display of remarkable powers, would it be possible to borrow from you the sum of twenty American dollars, just as a token of friendship?" the barker asked.

"I'm going to kill you both," Almayo said.

They looked at each other in stunned silence.

"Didn't you see me float above the ground?" the old man asked anxiously.

"You cheat," Almayo said. "I've seen hundreds like you. You cheap trash . . ."

"Good gracious," the old man said, in panic. "It didn't work. It's terrible. It's terrible. I'm losing my powers completely."

The barker sat very pale, his mouth twisted, watching the gun in Almayo's hand.

"Young man," he said in a trembling voice, "my friend here is willing to try again. Perhaps if you'd care to remove your gun . . . The conditions aren't perfect."

No, Almayo thought, he was not going to shoot them.

They deserved to stay alive, to stick to the muddy earth, to crawl on it. They were men, poor little men, trying to pretend, trying to create some illusion, more for their own sake than for the sake of others, to hide their meaninglessness, their nothingness, to give some mystery to their ordinary, suffering, creeping lives. He turned his back on them and walked out, grabbed the balustrade, and staggered down the stairs. From the bar they watched him cross the lobby and walk out into the bright, dazzling sunlight. He stood a moment dazed in the blinding light. His bodyguards were gone. They were still clinging to life and to whatever it had to offer.

Then he saw the American girl in front of him.

He had some difficulty in focusing his eyes, in the blinding light of noon, with the earth swaying under him and trying to throw him. At first he didn't believe it. But then he heard her voice and recognized its unbearable sweetness and warmth and in her eyes he saw once more the sickening goodness and the stubborn willingness to save him.

"Please, darling, please," she was saying. "You must listen to me. You must give yourself up. I'll be with you. I'll help you. I will tell them . . . Please, José, you have done so much for this country. There will be a trial—a public hearing—you will be acquitted. . . ."

He groaned and pulled out his gun.

"Please, let's not start a fight now, José," she was saying. "We still need each other. Believe me, it will be all right. . . ."

But he was not going to kill her. He was going to leave her behind, get rid of her once and for all, he was not going to take her with him. If he killed her, she would ruin him forever. She had it in her; she would plead relentlessly, in that sweet voice of hers, and tell them about the roads and the telephone and the Public Library, and he knew that she would convince them and drag him with her into Heaven.

She was crying now.

"Oh, my darling," she sobbed. "My poor darling, you are such a sad, confused boy!"

He got scared, and, as the world danced faster and faster around him, a cold shiver ran down his spine, for he could quite clearly hear the Heavenly choirs.

He shouted something and began to run.

It seemed to him that he had been running for hours, but those who dared to look only saw the Cujon stagger away from the girl and drag himself along the street and into the public square, with the gun in his hand. He recognized the familiar bandstand of all the small cities of the land, and stood there waiting for them to shoot, to kill him so that he could fulfill his longing and speak to him, see him at last with his own eyes, the True One, not some human fake, tell him everything he had done, and strike a bargain, and then return to earth and possess it truly and all the good things it had to offer.

Then it happened. He saw the dust dance under a thousand whips around him, and he felt the whiplash across his chest, and stood there for a while, his head lifted, his hands outstretched, and then another stroke of the whip hit him. He fell down, but he was still alive and still smiling, and his eyes were still searching the sky and the pain was smaller than the hope.

There was a silence, and then from the rooftops behind the machine guns the soldiers saw that the dog, after all, was not without a friend.

A man ran toward the body, his hands held high above his head in a sign of surrender, bent double in fear, but still running, in a strange, almost dancing way, turning loops in the dust to show to all that his arms were up and that he was surrendering; but then edging his way a little closer toward Almayo, turning another little loop, his face distorted in a horrified and imploring smile, holding his hands even higher to show that he meant no harm, and then, in the last edging little sideways run, he reached Almayo at last, and knelt by him.

Díaz was crying. He was scared as he had never been before, and yet his old charlatan's heart, his deep love of fakery, his need to cheat once more a man who was dying and therefore ready to believe as never before, gave him the courage to risk his life, and to reach Almayo to perform for him a last reassuring trick.

As he knelt by his side, his head shaking and his eyes jumping around in fear, holding his arms up, he managed to speak in a high, quivering voice: "You'll be all right, José. Just a few seconds more, and it will be all yours. You have made it. You will go straight to hell, and you will meet him and you will be back here in no time."

The Cujon nodded gravely.

"Okay," he said. "I know. I'll be okay."

The soldiers were running toward them and Díaz once more made a frantic gesture, trying to raise his outstretched arms even higher. His black-dyed hair was soiled with dust, and every inch of his face was shaking. He tried to make no move at all, for a nervous soldier could easily pull the trigger, and yet his own old, deep longing made him say in a reassuring voice: "Not a thing to worry about. You have made it. You have made yourself a deal. They'll buy it from you."

He knew himself that he was lying, but he also knew that he would never be found out. In fact, it was the only time in his whole life as an illusionist that he was sure he would never be found out. It was, in a way, a moment of triumph. He was beating them all, at last, all the great magicians that had ever lived, and no one would ever find out what he was hiding up his sleeve, for the promise of hell or of paradise is the only moment in his whole career when a charlatan can feel completely secure.

The soldiers were standing around them, silent, waiting for the dog to give up his last. The officer still held his gun pointed, but it was almost as a matter of courtesy toward the great fallen bandit.

"How did they know I was coming here?" Almayo murmured.

"I betrayed you," Díaz answered quickly and excitedly. "I have always been betraying you."

Almayo nodded in approval.

"Good," he murmured. "You really . . . do your best . . ."

"I work real hard," Díaz said, smiling through his tears. "Tell them. I've done the worst all my life, just to be sure."

Almayo's eyes were closing and his lips were quite white.

"You are getting there," Díaz said quickly. "You are almost there. Now you can see him. Now you can see him . . . now he's coming to welcome you. . . ."

He dared to bring one arm down and put it almost lovingly around Almayo's shoulders.

"You've made it, boy."

He was sobbing now, he was sobbing in longing and in hope and in disbelief. He could cheat the others, but he couldn't cheat himself. The old world was a brightly lit place without a shadow of mystery and the old, creeping suspicion that men were alone and masters of their fate filled him with an utmost misery and gave his tears a sincerity that he could hardly bear.

A disheveled, sobbing girl stumbled into the Hotel Flores and ran toward the man behind the counter.

"Please, please," she said, "get me the American Embassy at once."

The owner stared at her for one sad, pitying moment, then dialed the emergency number and handed the receiver to her. The girl took it and then, as she began to speak, she looked with a curious satisfaction at the telephone, and smiled.

The horses followed the trail around the mountain slope, into the valley, and under the setting sun.

The young evangelist was experiencing a strange and disturbing sensation entirely new to him. It was a sensation of emptiness that was spreading from under his heart and, reaching his throat, made him swallow hard. He was so completely exhausted and lost, the horrors of the last twenty-four hours had been of such unprecedented strangeness, so confused were his feelings and his thoughts, he was so prepared for some new and ghastly devilry, that it took him some effort to shake off his suspicion and regain enough of his senses to recognize this suddenly familiar sensation: he was simply very hungry. He laughed for the first time in a long, long while and looked around him with a sudden elation and pleasure; he felt somehow a different and, curiously enough, less serious and even less dedicated man; perhaps it would be better, he thought, if from now on he talked less to masses and more to individual people, to the lonely, the isolated, the lost; perhaps it would be better to have more friendly chats and fewer speeches; less thunder in his voice and more pity in his heart, and although he was still as determined as ever to carry on his crusade against evil, it would be better, perhaps, to speak of what men could do for each other, than to crush them under the flaming evocation of their ungodliness; to learn some tolerance from God and perhaps bother Him less, leave Him some peace, stop clinging to His name and start treating Him as tolerantly as if He were human too. He even looked at that unfortunate Cuban creature who rode beside him and had seldom left his side, as if he were placing himself under his protection, with a benevolent and forgiving eye; it was not the poor fellow's fault if he had been blessed—cursed, that is, Dr. Horwat corrected himself quickly—with that peculiar talent of his; and then it was only understandable that a man on this earth would dedicate himself to what he could do best, and eke out a living somehow. The truth was that young Dr. Horwat was completely punch-happy.

The Indian woman riding behind him fitted better into the landscape than any of them; she rolled gently in her saddle; an eternal silhouette of the land, and with that closed face of mystery which meant nothing but the total mastala-induced stupor; the evangelist decided that there was actually nothing wrong in this; under the circumstances, any doctor would have prescribed some similar drug anyway, and he even wondered if he shouldn't ask her for some mastala leaves himself.

The lawyer was thinking how complicated it was going to be to terminate José Almayo's earthly affairs and liquidate his holdings, bank accounts and business interests; he didn't know at all with whom he would have to deal, whom he should contact about it—and this last thought suddenly sent a slight shudder down his spine. It was not perhaps the safest thing for a man's soul, to be a great corporation lawyer; and perhaps the power and the wealth which his knowledge and ability protected so well were not the highest peak of achievement from which even the most honest lawyer could look around him with a clear conscience.

The Spanish girl's profile against the sky was as calm and mysterious as the sky itself and Otto Radetzky, who rode beside her and who didn't even know if she had truly noticed him, or if she would remember him tomorrow, was thinking that there was after all a true magic in this world, and that mankind had been blessed with a talent that lay too often wasted and forgotten in its heart.

The Baron was dozing in his saddle. Nothing had ever happened that could astonish or dismay him, and he knew that men still had a long way to go before they could become true artists, inspired and free creators of themselves, and of their own dignity; it required genius, and there was very little hope that they would achieve their greatness in his lifetime; but he was prepared to give them a chance and to circle the globe in his endless search, under his disguise of total indifference and under his mask of absence, forever watchful for the slightest manifestation of a true talent around him.

Charlie Kuhn was sitting on a horse for the first time in his life, and he was hardly in a mood to enjoy the experience. It was safer to avoid the road, but he was in a hurry and he was asking himself if the planes were leaving the country, or if he would have perhaps to wait for several days. He had heard about a few acts just before he came, and now he was eager to catch them before any of the other talent scouts got hold of them. There was an interesting magician in Havana—nothing really very different, but the man sounded good—and there was that fellow in Madras who could be pierced in twenty places, not with pins, like they all can, but with daggers, and without a drop of blood showing—a most promising act, if it proved true, for he was long accustomed to fantastic claims of human greatness. But he was always willing to take a good look—in fact, he was determined to keep looking as long as his heart would last, and perhaps even a little longer.

Monsieur Antoine sat firmly on his horse, good-humoredly juggling with three pebbles. Somehow, the craving for the impossible, for an absolute and unprecedented mastery, had abandoned him, and he was content to be merely alive, for he had learned that this was already a difficult feat and men were not very good at it, and in the end always failed.

"What is death?" the dummy Ole Jensen was saying, staring into the blue sky. "Nothing but a lack of talent."

On his miniature fiddle the musical clown was playing a sad little Jewish tune.

ABOUT THE AUTHOR

Romain Gary, the distinguished writer, soldier and diplomat, had his first novel, *A European Education*, published in France in 1945. It won the Prix des Critiques in 1945, became a best seller throughout Europe, and was finally published in a new and revised version in the United States in 1959. He followed with *Tulipe, The Company of Men*, and *The Colors of the Day*; and his fifth novel, *The Roots of Heaven*, won the Prix Goncourt, the top French literary honor. It sold over 300,000 copies in France and became an outstanding critical and popular success in England and America. Like several other of Mr. Gary's novels, it also became a motion picture. After *The Roots of Heaven, Lady L* became an international success. In April, 1960, the autobiographical volume *La Promesse de l'Aube* was published with outstanding success in France, and it is to be published in the United States and England late in 1961 after the novel, *The Talent Scout*, which was called *Le Mangeur d'Etoiles* in France. Mr. Gary's military career started with his enlistment in 1937 in the French Air Force, in which he served until the Fall of France. He then joined the R.A.F. in Great Britain, and eventually fought with the Free French. He was decorated with the Croix de la Liberation, the Croix de Guerre, and was also made a Chevalier of the Légion d'Honneur.

Mr. Gary's service as a career diplomat has included positions in the French embassies in England, Bulgaria and Switzerland. He served as First Secretary of the

French Delegation to the United Nations in New York. For over two years he was French Consul-General in Los Angeles, leaving the post in the summer of 1960 to return to Paris.

He was born of Russian ancestry in 1914, holds a law degree and speaks and writes French, English, Russian and Polish, with equal fluency. His wife is the English author Lesley Blanch.

Set in Linotype Janson
Format by Jean Krulis
Manufactured by The Haddon Craftsmen, Inc.
Published by HARPER & BROTHERS, *New York*